I0714724

HEATH HARKNESS

AND THE IMMORTALITY PLOT

W.D. MANKO

CK Books Publishing

Publisher's Cataloging-in-Publication Data
Names: Manko, W.D., author.
Title: Heath Harkness and the immortality plot / W.D. Manko.
Description: New Glarus, WI : CKBooks Publishing, 2021. | Series: Heath Harkness, vol. 1. | Summary: Heath tries to uncover a plot to steal the 2016 presidential election by a Transylvanian oligarch. | Audience: Grades 6 & up.
Identifiers: ISBN 978-1-949085-46-4 (paperback)
Subjects: LCSH: Young adult fiction. | MESH: Vampires--Fiction. | Conspiracies--Fiction. | Elections--Fiction. | Supernatural--Fiction. | Suspense fiction. | BISAC: YOUNG ADULT FICTION / Vampires. | YOUNG ADULT FICTION / Paranormal, Occult & Supernatural. | YOUNG ADULT FICTION / Thrillers & Suspense / Supernatural.
Classification: LCC PZ7.1.M36 He 2021 (print) | LCC PZ7.1.M36 (ebook) | DDC [Fic]--dc23.

LCCN: 2021924159

CKBooks Publishing
PO Box 214
New Glarus, WI 53574
◆ ckbookspublishing.com

Dedicated to the truth seekers
and the truth tellers

PROLOGUE

"You're quite sure this experiment will finally work? He won't end up like all the rest?" Dragomere Tepesh demanded of his son as the two of them peered intently through the large window separating their observation area from a sterile isolation room. On the other side of the glass, a brawny test subject wearing nothing but skimpy jogging shorts stood at rigid attention, his body bathed in the golden glow of simulated sunlight beaming down from the ceiling.

"It should work just fine, Father," Gregor Tepesh quickly replied. "Much better this time since we're recruiting better stock. This guy was the top athlete at his college and a former member of an elite military force before he joined our security service. According to all the preliminary tests, the new dosage amount is perfect."

"It better be," Dragomere Tepesh growled,

abruptly cutting off his son's nervous assurance. "The election is only months away. Time is what matters, not one puny life. This guy's expendable. Get on with it."

Gregor turned toward the lab-coated chemist standing near a control panel of knobs and levers and blinking lights. "Proceed with the test," he ordered.

The chemist nodded quickly and sprang forward to raise the strength of the sunshine-bright light one more notch.

A few moments later, the young man behind the glass shot his observers a cocky grin and raised his arms in mock body-builder posture to show off biceps slowly becoming more muscular.

Dragomere nodded his head in tentative approval. "So far, so good. Let's take it up one more level."

Gregor again relayed the order to the chemist. Hand shaking, the man turned the knob yet again, his nervous gaze reluctantly returning to the test subject. The husky young man's grin widened as he flexed muscles that bulged even more impressively beneath his sweat-bathed skin.

For a brief moment the test results appeared perfect – then all hell broke loose.

Dragomere's momentary satisfaction dissolved in a flash as he watched the man beyond the window stiffen in shocked surprise. Mere seconds later, the young man began to writhe, clawing frantically at the blood-red lesions suddenly appearing on his body.

Eyes filled with desperation, the man rushed toward the window. "Help me!" he begged.

But there was no help to be had.

In mere minutes, his flesh melted from his bones while he screamed in agony. Finally, his ravaged body crumbled to the floor, leaving little more than a puddle of gore and blood.

Father and son studied the scene beyond their window in tension-filled silence.

Seconds later, his anger barely controlled, Dragomere turned and glared at his son. "Well, I'd hardly call that perfect," he chastised. "What went wrong?"

"I-I don't know," Gregor stammered, beads of nervous sweat breaking out on his brow.

"I strongly suggest that you find out," snapped his father. "We're running out of time to establish a no-fail balance of the chemical formula and the level of light sensitivity. You know having ultra-enhanced members of the security team trained and in place before fall is absolutely essential to our plans."

"Yes, of course," Gregor replied, his shaved head bobbing in fawning agreement.

The elder Tepesh turned his rage on the

chemist cowering in the corner. "Don't just stand there! Have that mess cleaned up, then run another panel of computer analyses. I want a full-fledged test scheduled for next week when I return from the final campaign meeting in Waukesha."

"Y-Yes, sir. Of course, sir. I'll get to work on it immediately."

Grateful for his reprieve from some-thing more violent than his employer's tongue-lashing, the chemist shut down the control panel and made a hasty exit from the room.

CHAPTER
†
ONE

The air smelled purified, the aroma clean and pleasing after the fierce thunderstorm that had blanketed the city the night before. Twilight had spread its cloak over the McGovern home, which held a swarm of guests who had been invited to a return-to-school get-together for their daughter Zoe. A tantalizing array of refreshments filled the dining room table. Wine and beer were readily available, and the latest popular music played in the background. In a nearby nook, a number of people were hanging on every word uttered by a hired tarot card reader.

Heath Harkness grabbed a beer from a serving tray carried by one of the caterer's waitstaff as those who'd already received readings began to wander away. He took a quick swallow before flashing a grin at the pretty young woman by his side. "Okay, Zoe, your turn. Let's see what wonderful things the next semester has in store for you." Remembering the difficult months Zoe had recently experienced, Heath silently hoped the reading would offer his long-time friend something positive and uplifting.

The tarot reader quickly shuffled the deck then placed the cards face down on the table. Next, the woman reached out with crimson-tipped fingers to turn over the first card. She perused it for a moment. "Most auspicious, indeed," she murmured as she flashed a quick smile at Zoe. "I see a bright future. New experiences and new friends."

The knot in Heath's stomach shrank a bit. He watched intently as another card was turned and the woman spoke again. "This one shows success in education, and a new and exciting challenge coming your way."

The burgundy highlights in Zoe's dark hair glowed softly as she glanced up at Heath and, to his relief, offered a fair imitation of the sparkling smile he remembered from the past. Each new card turned brought another positive comment from the reader, which encouraged more smiles from Zoe. Heath breathed a soft sigh as worry eased in his mind.

"Your turn, Heath," Zoe declared when Heath started to lead her away from the table once the cards' glowing forecast for her was completed.

"Sure. Why not," he agreed. Anything to keep his friend smiling after being overwhelmed by sadness for far too many months. Having lost a member of his own family in a bizarre work accident a year before, Heath understood Zoe's downward spiral after the death of her older brother in a terrible car wreck. Heath had vivid memories of the depression she'd fallen into, an overwhelming despair that caused many of her friends to step back from the girl. But, much to Heath's relief, Zoe finally seemed to be doing better, and he was determined to do whatever he could to lift her spirits so her recovery would continue.

The reader gave the deck of cards another good shuffle, then once again placed a number of them face down on the table. She turned up the first card.

"That's . . . interesting," she murmured as she stared at the card before slowly laying it face up on the table.

Heath studied the odd picture on the card – screaming figures falling from a tall tower set against a dark background and surrounded by bold yellow flashes hinting of lightning and fire. "Interesting how?" he asked. "What's it mean?"

"Oh...uh...the Tower card predicts a change, perhaps even a threat of some sort. One you can meet with grace or . . ." Seeing Heath's perplexed look, the woman quickly ended her prediction. "Let's see what the next one shows," she said as she reached out and picked up a second card. She pulled in a quick breath when she turned it over to reveal a man hanging upside down.

Heath saw Zoe frown at the disturbing picture and quickly forced a cocky smile to his face and a lilt to his voice. "And that one means . . . ?"

The woman flicked a dismissive hand toward the card, as if eager to chase away the message it presented. "It can be interpreted in several different ways. It, too, could mean a change in your future, something inevitable." She shrugged her shoulders. "Whether great or small can't be easily deciphered."

The reader hesitated a long moment before reaching out to turn the third card over. "The Chariot," she said, a hint of relief in her voice. "A powerful card. Once again, this suggests a change, one that might be long and difficult, but it's a change that can instill strength of purpose in you and give you confidence that you can accomplish what you thought you could not."

Noticing the puzzled frown on Zoe's face, Heath quickly feigned approval, wondering if the tarot woman's hesitant pronouncements meant she was simply trying to fabricate a more positive response to keep his reading more in tune with the one she'd given Zoe.

"Tell me more," he commented in the most cheerful tone he could muster. He was rewarded with another smile from Zoe, more tentative than before, but at least she still seemed to be enjoying herself.

Another card was turned, revealing an armor-clad skeleton atop a horse. The fortune teller sat silent for a long moment. "That one is the ... uh, it's the ..." Then she abruptly halted without naming the card or giving any sort of an explanation. Snatching up another card, she quickly turned it over.

Heath gazed in dismay at what he saw – the devil, horned and evil-looking as he loomed over a shackled man and woman. He straightened and pasted on a nonchalant isn't-this-fun expression, hopeful that the woman would once again find a positive meaning for the disquieting picture.

The woman's chair wobbled and fell to the floor as she suddenly surged to her feet. "Oh! So sorry. I, uh, I suddenly feel quite ill. Please excuse me."

She swept the cards into a jumbled pile, grabbed them up, and almost ran from the room, leaving Heath speechless as he mentally scrambled for words that, for Zoe's sake, might put a positive spin on the bizarre incident.

ChAPTER

†

TWO

Bulging backpack slung over his shoulder, Heath took the college's creaky old stairs two at a time. It was the first day of his senior year – a year he believed would change his life in many ways, the first one being the new journalism class he was headed for. Taught by one of the country's most renowned newspaper men, Heath believed it would be a turning point in his life. He moved his Obamaesques body up the stairs with excitement. Dreams of success swirled in his head – opinion pieces, investigative articles, maybe even a book some day. As a successful writer, he hoped to provide an important service to more than his home city. His words might fuel challenges and encourage all sorts of people to better themselves and help others.

Heath's grin widened at the lofty thought. His father would have been so proud. Heath sobered as memories of the past crept in. Things had certainly changed for the Harkness family in the last few years.

After Heath's high school graduation, his family had moved to Dead Crow, Wisconsin, a small town an hour's drive southwest of Milwaukee, in pursuit of a better life. Using all their savings, his parents had bought their first house, a fixer-upper in the Lake Crest Development area, an older community not far from a small, isolated lake known locally as Green Gas Lake because of a strange mist that sometimes appeared over it at night. Outside the city limits and untended by any city agency, the lake was more than unappealing and was rarely visited by any of the town's citizens.

Shrugging off local gossip about possible illegal dumping and contamination in the area, Heath's father had applied for a job at Dragon Enterprises, a manufacturing plant on the shores of that stagnant little lake. Since its arrival in the city, the recently established company had generated quite a reputation. Much of what they did was hush-hush, but there'd been a flood of rumors about space-age technology and break-through chemical products from those who claimed to be privy to reliable resources.

Even more interesting to Arthur Harkness had been the news of impressive wages and substantial perks for employees of the company. A proud black man, he'd been much relieved at the swift offer of a job as an upper-echelon security officer. The promise of a fat paycheck was a godsend. It would allow Heath's mother, Mary, the sweet blue-eyed blonde from the other side of town that Arthur had wooed and won during their senior year of high school, to waitress only part-time.

Arthur had been prouder still of what he'd been able to finally guarantee for his son. With an offered scholarship from Parkwood College, a private institution founded by a group of nuns in the 1890s, supplemented by Heath's after-school job at a local bakery during his high school years, Arthur had felt assured that his son would receive a proper college education, something he himself regretted never having.

Heath's first two years at college had been wonderful, all that Heath and his family had wished they would be. Then, early in his junior year, everything had changed. A tragic work accident had taken the life of his father and forever changed their lives. Mary was working full-time again, and Heath was pouring all his energy into his classes, striving to keep the heart-felt promise he'd made on the day of his father's funeral service to earn that degree his father had looked forward to with such pride. Heath's hard work was paying off. He had earned high marks in all his junior-year classes as well as super-star status on the college's esteemed newspaper.

The sound of Heath's footsteps followed him down the long second-floor hallway until he reached the door to his classroom. The worn bronze doorknob turned easily, and the heavy door opened with a metallic click. Drawing a deep breath, Heath stepped inside and quickly began to scan the room for his friends. His gaze found Zoe just as she turned, smiled enthusiastically, and pointed at the chair on her right, indicating she'd saved a seat for him. David Abraham, a double major in journalism and IT, and Heath's colleague from last semester's debate class, occupied the seat on Zoe's left.

Relieved that his new professor was nowhere in sight to witness his late arrival, Heath hastened to claim his place.

David nodded in greeting, sending longish brown hair swaying as Heath slipped into the empty chair. "Hey, buddy. Have you heard the gossip yet?" he asked in a carefully lowered voice. The scraggly tuft of beard on his chin danced with cach uttered word.

"What gossip?" Heath softly replied as he wiggled out of his backpack and dumped it on the hardwood floor.

"Rumor has it that Professor Stein's gonna have some really big announcement to make. Couldn't get a whiff of what, but folks are pretty juiced."

"I heard he won some big prize for his article on Afghanistan a couple years ago," Heath offered. "Maybe he's got some new commendation to tell us about."

David shrugged. "Dunno. There's lots of wild speculation going on."

Just as Heath opened his mouth to respond, a door in the teacher's area of the room opened and the professor strode in.

Tall, with an athletic build, the attractive middle-aged man sauntered to the over-sized desk at the front of the room and deposited the abundance of books and file folders in his arms. After placing the last item, a shiny expensive looking iPad, carefully on top of the stack, the professor straightened and shrugged off his stylish suit coat, hanging it on the back of the antique wooden chair behind the desk. He straightened and squared his shoulders. Then, hands clasped behind his back, he eyed the gathering of suddenly hushed students.

"Good morning, ladies and gentlemen. I'm Jacob Stein, Jack for short, Investigative Reporter for the *New York Times*, and newly sanctioned professor here at Parkwood College."

The low buzz of conversation among students quickly fell silent as the professor's dark gaze slowly swept the classroom as though he were evaluating each and every one of them. Finally, he swiped a hand over his graying hair and nodded. "I'm delighted to have been offered the opportunity to spearhead this new course in my favorite area of reporting. My goal is to teach you how to really dig into your investigative research, how to effectively analyze the people you will interview, and how to apply what you learn to ferret out truth. Truth that might make our lives, our communities, perhaps even our government, better and safer for the continued protection of this country's people."

Interesting. Meaty and different from the usual who-what-when-where-and-how we've been lectured on so often, thought Heath as he exchanged approving nods with his seatmates.

"This class will initiate you into the challenges of pursuing the truth in an environment growing more hostile to it," Jack Stein continued. "My goal is to instill dedication and determination into those of you who believe in facts as much as I do."

Eager hands began to shoot upward.

"Let's save those questions for a little later," the

professor stated. "Let's get acquainted first. Tell me your name and your major and—"

The screech of the classroom door opening interrupted Jack Stein's instructions.

Oops, some poor schmuck later than me, Heath thought as he automatically turned his head to look. All speculation of whether the interruption would garner rebuke for tardiness from the professor vanished as he watched one of the most beautiful women he'd ever seen slip into the room. His mind barely acknowledged a waterfall of long black hair and emerald-green eyes before zeroing in on a body fit for a career in modeling.

Heath's jaw dropped and he watched in fascination as the girl walked toward him. She moved with the grace of a runway model, her short skirt of silky fabric in an evocative shade of smoky blue rippling against tanned legs that seemed to go on forever. He could hardly believe his luck when she paused at the unoccupied desk next to his and then gracefully took a seat.

He wasn't the only one in the room staring at the new student. A quick glance around the room revealed men apparently as transfixed as he was with the sight of the unexpected goddess in their midst.

"Oh, my god," Zoe snapped under her breath. "Close your mouth before you drool all over yourself."

A flash of heat climbed Heath's checks. "Sorry," he muttered, wondering why Zoe was so irritated with him.

The question vanished from his mind when the new student ran the tip of her tongue over cherry-colored lips and then began to speak in a sultry voice that sent shivers down Heath's spine.

"I'm sorry," she hastened to explain to the professor. "I'm new to the campus and I got lost trying to find the classroom."

"Ah, you must be the transfer student from Hamilton the dean told me about," Professor Stein remarked. "What brings you to Dead Crow and Parkwood College?"

"A family situation," the new girl answered with an accompanying sigh. "My mother's been having some . . . uh, some health problems, and my father decided he wanted me to attend a school closer to the family."

An off-tone in her words pulled Heath's attention from her physical attributes and brought a question to his mind. Was that simple irritation at the inconvenience of an unexpected move, or was she ticked at her dad for messing in her life? The professor hesitated so long before responding that Heath wondered if he'd picked up on the same tone.

"Well, the students were just getting acquainted," Stein said, deftly ignoring the testy-sound of the girl's reply. "Why don't you go first? Tell us your name and what you're majoring in, please," he instructed.

Rising to stand beside her desk, the new girl nervously flipped a swath of long curls over her shapely shoulder and away from her face before replying. "I'm Victoria Tepesh. Actually, I'm a business major but I thought this class might be an interesting elective."

Stein froze for a fraction of a second then seemed to shake himself loose. "Thank you, Miss Tepesh."

Tepesh? The name scratched at a fleeting memory in Heath's mind, but the question of exactly what that memory was skittered away as he watched the young lady reclaim her chair then slowly cross one long leg over the other. Heath's breath caught in his throat as the short skirt she was wearing inched higher.

Zoe muttered something unrecognizable under her breath, and Heath quickly averted his gaze, doing his best to drag his full attention back to the professor, who was beginning to speak again.

"Thank you," Professor Stein said as he shifted his weight and turned toward the far side of the room. "Next, let's begin with the gentleman in the red tee-shirt. Your name and major, if you please."

The introductions continued with great speed as, row by row, the students stood and identified themselves and the subject they were majoring in.

Heath's answer didn't ring as clear as Zoe's and David's. Still hyper-aware of the stunning new student, he was relieved that he'd at least managed to give his response without stumbling over the words.

Once again, Professor Stein clasped his hands behind his back, rocked on his heels for a few seconds, and then began a slow amble back and forth in front of his desk. "By now, some of you may have heard hints about the new course work. I hope you'll all be excited by what I've formulated for the class."

Murmurs of interest began to ripple through the room.

The professor continued. "We're going to start this semester off with a special assignment, one that could take some of you months to complete but which will be well worth your time and effort. You're going to be down in the ditches, digging up facts, facts that could impact our city and our country for years to come."

Stein ceased his pacing. Facing the classroom, he slid his hands into his trouser pockets before continuing his announcement. "This task, this *challenge*, will garner a full one-third of your final class score. It will also earn you the most vital experience in the field of Journalism that you could ever imagine. Be assured that I will work with each and every one of you, providing individual guidance and direction on the appropriateness of your chosen subject as necessary. The sign-up sheet is right here," he said, placing a piece of paper on the corner of his desk. "Be sure to sign up and pick a preferred time for your consultation before you leave class."

The professor paused and perused his students. "Now, back to the details of the assignment. The first part is easy. I want you to consider several subjects for your interview. Analyze them as you look for a person of real importance, someone with real impact – good or bad -- on the world around them." His shoulders lifted in a theatrical shrug. "Could be a renowned church dignitary, a vision-inspired inventor, maybe even an outstanding business leader. Take some time to think about this. When you've decided on your target interview candidate, we'll go over your choice in individual meetings. My goal is to make sure you're not wasting time on the wrong person."

"What about politicians?" a geeky young man on the far side of the room asked.

"Excellent thinking." the professor agreed. "The presidential election is just months away. Trouble often brews in government. Just think what happened when Hitler took over Germany. Concentration camps, death chambers, the brutal murder of millions of innocent people–"

"That could never happen here," a student commented.

Stein shook his head. "Don't be so sure of that. There are rumors out there right now about questionable people who have ties to various governing bodies right here in the USA. Why, I heard one just the other day about the governor of our fair state getting himself elected with more than a little help from an elusive billionaire who just happens to have ties to this town. No telling what an investigative reporter with a little gumption could come up with. So keep an open mind. There are a lot of people to consider – good people, bad people, people wealthy enough to impact lives in many ways."

For the first time since the new student's arrival, Professor Stein had Heath's full attention. Stein's comment had sparked another flash of memory, and Heath was suddenly dead-set certain he didn't need any prolonged discussion with the new professor. He already knew exactly who he wanted to interview, the multi-billionaire shadow-man who owned Dragon Enterprises and often slipped quietly into town to oversee his latest business venture, and then out again like a ghost. The man who'd sent flowers for Arthur Harkness's funeral but hadn't bothered to attend. The man who'd never sufficiently answered Mary and Heath's questions about the accident that had taken their loved one's life, an accident so tragic that the funeral service had been closed casket.

Backed by the hallowed entity of Parkwood and the perfect excuse to probe provided by his new, much renowned professor's curriculum, Heath was positive he'd finally found a way to get answers to the questions that had plagued him and his mother since his father's death.

CHAPTER
†
THREE

Determined to win Stein's approval of his proposed candidate for the big interview assignment, Heath signed up for one of the first offered consultation slots before he left class that first day. To ensure readiness for the discussion regarding his choice, he spent every moment of free time he could snatch the rest of the week working on the argument he would present to the professor.

Despite all his preparation, there was a flutter of apprehension in the pit of his stomach as he approached Stein's office on the day of his appointment.

Normally, he would have shared his thoughts with Zoe, maybe even practiced his debatable points with her, but he hadn't been able to reach her for one of their usual gab sessions all week, and she hadn't responded to any of the messages he'd left. Hitting the local college hangout on Saturday night in hopes of running into her or David – or maybe the new girl in class – had crossed his mind, but he'd quickly chased the thought away. Winning approval of his plan was more important. His time would be better spent polishing his presentation.

Now, faced with the final challenge of all his preparation, Heath hesitated a moment, wondering what his odds were. Behind the door's frosted glass, a shadow of movement caught his attention. Time to take the leap.

Drawing in a deep breath, Heath squared his shoulders and knocked on the professor's office door. A muffled male voice called, "Come in."

"Good morning," Professor Stein greeted as the door swung open.

Heath hesitated in the doorway for just a moment, then stepped into the small room crowded with bookcases and file cabinets. A pale shaft of sunlight speared through a small curtainless window.

"Good morning, sir," Heath said, the quiver in his voice betraying his nervousness.

The professor pointed at the guest chair in front of his desk. "Have a seat and tell me who you're thinking about interviewing and why."

Folding his six-foot frame into the small armchair, Heath swiped his damp palms on the knees of his best pair of jeans. Mental fingers crossed, he presented the first sentence of his carefully crafted argument.

The words had barely been spoken when Stein's welcoming smile vanished. Leaning back in his chair, the professor scrutinized Heath for a long moment. "Tepesh, huh?"

Heath gave a nervous nod and wondered if he'd stumbled into a no-win situation. Was he about to be shot down before he even had a chance to explain?

Holy hell. What if Stein and Tepesh were cronies, best buddies? The thought wasn't too far-fetched. As a prize-winning reporter, Stein had rubbed shoulders with all kinds of people. One of them could easily have been Dragon Enterprises' president.

"Approved," Stein said.

Surprise flooded through Heath. He'd come prepared for a battle and there hadn't even been a skirmish.

"Uh, thanks," he managed to say. He'd never considered such a fast capitulation. He scooted forward in the chair, hoping the professor would wrap things up quickly so he could make a quick escape. "I . . . uh, I guess you already know him?"

Stein shook his head. "Not really. I've never met him but I know *of* him. What made you decide on him as your candidate?"

Heath considered answering with some of the scholarly points he'd prepared, but suddenly decided on the truth. "The girl . . . uh, the new student. When she told us her name, it rang a bell. It took me a little while, but I finally figured it out."

"Ah," Stein replied, his eyes bright with interest. "You thought she might provide a means of access to her father?"

Heath shook his head. "No, that didn't even cross my mind. Something about her last name was familiar. It kept bugging me, and finally, I remembered. I could even see a picture of that name in my mind . . . bold black letters on a small white card attached to one of the wreaths at my father's funeral. Dragomere Tepesh. No message, just the signature of the very rich man who owns the company where my father died almost two years ago."

A look of surprise flashed across Stein's face. He shook himself free of the shock and leaned forward as if to reach out to Heath. "Died? How terrible for you. I'm so sorry."

Emotions and memories swirling, Heath locked his gaze on the glass globe paperweight on Stein's desk and just kept talking. "We never heard from Tepesh or any other officer of the company.

The only person we – my mother and me – were ever able to talk to was his secretary. She told Mom that OSHA had investigated the accident and found the company not at fault, that my dad had simply been the victim of an unfortunate industrial accident. That was it. The next time we called, the receptionist told us the woman had been transferred to another company Tepesh owns in another state."

"Outrageous," the professor muttered.

A tight lump had formed in Heath's throat. He swallowed hard and plowed ahead, determined to finish the tale. "We kept trying, but we could never get through to anyone else. We left messages, but no one called back. And no one from the company attended the funeral. A fair-sized check marked 'death benefits' arrived in our home mail several weeks later, and that was the end of it."

Stein shook his head. "I'm so sorry. I can't even imagine how tough that was for your family."

Heath gave himself a mental shake and straightened in the chair, ready to defend his choice for interview if necessary. Something in Stein's attentive demeanor told him it was time to get back to his presentation and all the logical reasons he'd worked so hard to develop. "I . . . uh, well, as to my reason for picking him, let me explain–"

Stein waved a hand in dismissal. "I get it, and I totally agree. There're more and more people like

Tepesh nowadays. Our whole government system seems to be going to hell in a handbasket. We've got lobbyists and billionaires showering private enterprise and governments, local, state, and federal, with huge bribes and donations in order to get what they want, be that avoiding fault for wrong doings or looking to lock in land or water rights or access to oil pipelines, and rights-of-way that the general population doesn't want but some rich ol' guy does 'cause he's greedy for more money. Damn oligarchs believe they can buy whatever the hell they want." Stein sighed. "And chances are they're right. Government for the rich, the few, not the people or the country."

Heath was surprised and impressed by his professor's passionate comments. The man was obviously brilliant. Almost instantly Stein had seen how emphasis could shift from a family tragedy to something of much broader impact. No wonder he'd had so many front-page stories during his career. Encouraged, Heath shared another thought that had plagued him since his father's death. "Rich as Tepesh is rumored to be, I always wondered if they'd bribed someone to cover up the cause of the accident."

The professor nodded vigorously. "Very possible. Wouldn't be the first time and probably won't be the last if someone doesn't step up to put a stop to such travesties of justice."

"Exactly," Heath agreed, feeling vindicated and encouraged for the first time in a long while. "But won't it be hard to get to genuine information? If Tepesh was good enough to buy himself out of trouble once, he can probably do it again. They stonewalled us before. I figure they'll do it on additional inquires."

"Not to worry, Mr. Harkness. That's what this class is for – to train new journalists in the skills needed to get to the truth, to see that bigger picture. That's why I proposed this part of the curriculum to the college. I'm delighted to have you onboard."

Heath grinned. "Sounds good to me, sir. I hope to put all that I learn from you to good use one day."

Brow furrowed in thought, the professor glanced at his watch, then settled back in his chair to study Heath for a long moment. "Why wait for 'one day'?" he asked. "Why not start working on such problems right now?"

Not quite sure where the professor was going with the subject but intrigued with what he might have to say, Heath leaned forward, hands clasped between his knees. "How?"

"We could put together a small, hand-picked group of students – those who are *really* interested in tackling some of these issues, not afraid to do a little prying – maybe even some spying – to find out the truth. The smartest, most dedicated students in the class." His face a picture of determination, Stein continued. "We'd need to pick participants carefully. We'd meet after school hours for discussions, debates, maybe even guest speakers. Members of the group could get some hands-on practice with the investigative tools available to us in this high-tech age. Who knows – if they're brave enough, determined enough, there might be a chance to make an impact on what seems to be going wrong in the world and benefit society. How does that sound?"

Stein had Heath's full attention. "That sounds amazing."

"We could start right here and bring a light to the missteps in justice that are happening locally, maybe even look into what's going on in the state. With the right kind of people ferreting out the truth and getting the word out, we might make a difference. Are you interested?"

Head spinning with the possibilities, Heath nodded. "Absolutely."

Professor Stein smiled. "Excellent. Can you think of any other students who'd fit our requirements who might be interested?"

"Sure. Zoe and David would be perfect. We've had lots of discussions on various business and political problems, and we all agree something needs to be done. We just don't know where to start."

The professor smiled. "Well, now you do. All

we need is the right mix of students. David and Zoe are good candidates. We'll invite them to join the group. And you can be on the lookout for anyone else who'd fit in."

"Well, I can think of a couple of students who are big into politics and problems within our social services, but they aren't in our class."

"No problem," Stein assured with a wave of his hand. "This special group won't be officially connected to the journalism class. A good mix of people from different walks of life might be very useful. Keep that in mind as you consider candidates."

"Yes, sir. I can do that."

Stein stilled. Deep in thought, he scratched at his chin. "What do you think about inviting Victoria Tepesh to join the group?"

Heath perked up. He wasn't sure how much was because of her connection to his own father's former employer or the fact that having her in the group would provide a chance to get to know her better. He had no idea if Victoria Tepesh would say yes, but if he handled the invitation carefully and kept his mouth shut about his own personal interest, maybe, just maybe, she would.

Heath's mind wandered back to the tone of disdain he thought he'd heard in her voice that first day in class. A wishful thought followed. If he was right and she was genuinely angry at her dad, he could only hope the reason was something really reprehensible. Something bad enough to make his daughter willing to help the group.

"Excellent idea, sir," he told the professor.

Stein smiled. "Perfect. Think about what friends you might want to talk to, and keep me informed. The other item that needs to be addressed is finding a good place to meet. Since the group won't be officially connected with the class, I think we need somewhere we can talk freely and exchange ideas about possible ways we might solve problems if we do find anything amiss. A place conducive to frank discussion and analysis of possible solutions. A place where we won't be disturbed or overheard."

"Makes sense," Heath said, his mind already clicking through locations that might fit the professor's requirements.

Stein paused and then raised a finger. "One more thing. We need to keep the group secret, so it's important to consider each person's ability to do that before you invite them to participate. No sense taking any chances on gossip that might get back to some of the people we might want to check out."

Heath nodded understanding.

The professor looked pleased. "The right people, the right methods. No telling what we might turn up."

CHΛPTER
†
FOUR

Heath paced the back corner of the college library, a nook stocked with bound copies of former students' dissertations that seldom lured anyone to visit. He'd texted Zoe and David the day after his meeting with Stein, asking them to meet him there after their last classes. Both had texted back in the affirmative.

Since he didn't know Victoria Tepesh's cell number, he'd watched for an opportunity to slip her a short note he'd prepared the previous evening as they passed in the hall between classes. He had no idea if she'd show up.

Deep in thought as he rounded the end of a row of bookcases and started up another aisle, Heath didn't notice Zoe coming up behind him. He jumped in surprise when she tapped him on the shoulder.

Relieved that someone had actually shown up, he bent to give her a hug and asked her to join him where a small table with two chairs on each side sat unoccupied.

A big smile on her face, Zoe willingly followed.

Heath pulled out a chair for Zoe and then snagged the chair next to her for himself. Once settled, he turned to face his classmate, bending toward her to quietly ask, "Did you happen to spot David as you came in?"

Following Heath's lead, Zoe kept her voice low when she answered. "Nope, but I saw him at lunch and he said he'd be here."

Placing an elbow on the table's polished walnut surface, she propped her chin in her hand and turned inquisitive eyes on Heath. "So, what's with the cloak and dagger stuff?"

Heath shook his head. "Let's wait till David gets here. It'll be easier if I explain it to everyone at the same time."

"Whatever you say," Zoe agreed.

An impish grin on her face, she leaned in closer to Heath and nervously ran her fingers through the riot of burgundy curls swinging over her shoulder. "Have, uh, have you seen that new movie at the Rialto yet? I've heard good things about it and I wondered if you'd like to–"

David's arrival stopped her mid-sentence.

"Okay, guys, the gang's all here. Let's get this party started." He plopped his bulging backpack down on the table and folded his lanky frame into one of the two empty chairs on the other side. "So, what's this big news you've got for us?"

Heath was too busy sneaking one last look down the aisle to notice the frustration that flashed across Zoe's face at the interruption.

"Well, all right. Looks like we're it," Heath muttered, a hint of disappointment in his voice. "So, here's the deal. I met with Professor Stein yesterday to talk about my choice for that special interview assignment, and after he approved my choice, he brought up something else–"

"You got approved already?" David asked. "How the heck did you do that?"

"Well, I–" Heath began.

"Sorry I'm late."

The smile on Zoe's face evaporated at the sound of Victoria Tepesh's voice. Heath noted that Zoe quickly turned her attention to finding something in her purse, apparently no longer interested in what he'd been telling David about his visit with the professor. All too busy welcoming Victoria, he didn't notice Zoe's disappointed sigh or the fact that she quickly straightened so that there was more distance between the two of them.

Oblivious to Zoe's sudden silence and David's

subsequent perusal of the interaction between the two of them, Heath forgot all about the explanation he'd started to provide and greeted the newcomer with a big smile. "I'm so glad you could make it," he told Victoria.

"Thanks," Victoria replied, wiggling out of the pale green jacket she was wearing. Draping the jacket on the back of the empty chair, she claimed the last place at the table.

Heath pulled his cell phone from his pocket and pushed it across the table. "Uh, before we get started, how about punching your cell number into my phone? That way I can send text messages to everyone. It'll be, uh, more convenient."

"Sure." Victoria picked up the phone and began to tap in her number.

Studiously ignoring Victoria's busy fingers, Zoe ducked her head and began to fiddle with the silver ring adorning her right hand.

David quickly turned his attention back to Heath, filling the awkward silence. "We can discuss your jiffy approval by Stein later. Tell us about the big news you just hinted at."

Heath pulled his lengthy gaze from Victoria. "Uh, I was just explaining that Professor Stein suggested something else at the meeting we had with him. Something I think is well worth participating in." Eager that his three listeners would feel the same interest in the proposal that he had, he quickly outlined Stein's idea.

"What do you think?" he asked when he'd finished.

David tugged at his shaggy beard then nodded in agreement. "It could be fun. I wouldn't mind getting some more experience with those new investigative gadgets I'm experimenting with. Could look good on my resume after graduation."

A determined look on her face, Zoe cut a quick sideways glance at Heath. "I'm in."

Victoria sighed. "It's too bad participation in the group won't offer a chance at better grades, which might help get my father off my case. That would have been great. Still, the political angle could be helpful. That's all he ever talks about anymore. I'm so sick of hearing about new laws and how important business tax cuts are going to be after the next election, I could croak. I'd do just about anything to put an end to all the lectures on politics and proper ways to govern he's given me since I moved here."

"Your dad's involved in politics?" Heath asked, wondering if Tepesh's daughter had just presented him with the first hint that there might be some truth to his speculation about his father's accident and a possible bribe to cover something up. "In what way?"

Victoria made a face. "He's all involved with

the campaign for that governor who's running for president. You know, that Todd Walters. It's not fair for him to insist I move here when I have a great life in Manhattan, which is away from him and his robber-baron friends. Fortunately, it's just Mother and me at the house."

Eager for anything or anyone who might provide another clue in his quest for information, Heath pounced on the new name. "Who's Gregor?"

"My brother. He lives at home, too. Father put him in charge of some new-fangled product tests out at the new facility."

CHAPTER
†
FIVE

When Zoe arrived home, she went straight to her room where she dumped her backpack and purse on the small white desk in the far corner, stopping only long enough to unzip the stuffed-to-the-gills bag and remove her laptop.

The image of Heath going all calf-eyed at Victoria's arrival still lingered, leaving her frustrated and feeling the urgent need to intervene somehow. Heath was her closest friend, the guy who'd known exactly how to console her after her brother's death, the one person who could tease her out of the down times with just the right words. Somewhere in the last few months, she'd come to see him as something more than a friend. Now, the relationship that had slipped into her private thoughts was in jeopardy and she needed to find a way to protect it.

Ignoring the avalanche of books and papers that slid from the open maw of her backpack, she headed across the room and climbed atop her double bed to sit cross-legged on a white duvet splattered with purple hydrangeas. Once settled against a pile of throw pillows in various shades of purple, she balanced the computer on her lap and began to type.

"Tepesh" Zoe murmured as she tapped into her browser to look for ammunition of any sort, and not at all sure what she'd do with it if she found it.

"With a name like that, I should be able to find *something* on the Internet," she assured herself. She tried "Victoria Tepesh" first. Each click on a new website brought up only a morsel or two about the new girl.

After a while, Zoe shook her head in disbelief at how sparse the information was. A high school graduation list showing the names of the students. A very small article about Victoria Tepesh participating in a freshman class project at her original university. But nothing juicy.

Zoe nudged a pillow into a more comfortable position behind her back and tried Facebook. Nothing.

Pinterest. Nothing.

Each successive site for social media provided absolutely nothing. It didn't make any sense.

"Impossible," she muttered. "A prominent

college student without any social media information? That's too weird for words. She's like some flipping ghost."

Zoe paused and mentally scrolled through possible alternatives. "Well, if searching for the daughter doesn't work, then daddy dearest will have to do. What the heck was the name of the new company he's president of out by the lake? Dragon something? Company? No. Enterprises? Oh, yeah, that's it."

Cursor in the search bar, she quickly typed in the words, linking Tepesh and the company's name. A long list of available websites popped up. Determined to find something, Zoe continued to click away, searching any domain name that looked like it might lead to the kind of information she was seeking. After spending some time, an unfamiliar website caught her attention.

"This looks promising," she said, clicking on the link.

A long list of unfamiliar organization names popped up on her screen. She scrolled through it. Under "T" she found a small entry for "Tepesh."

Dragomere Tepesh, founder of Drago-mere Holdings, also referred to as DH Holdings. Born 1946 in Berlin, Germany. Oil speculator, international investor, and philanthro-

pist. President of new Dragon Enterprises corporation in Wisconsin. Married Helena Bishop in 1966. Two children.

"Well, that's the guy, but where's the detailed information about the kids? And all the pictures?" Zoe remarked in an irritated whisper. "There aren't any recent pictures, just a couple of old grainy ones. And there's nothing about his children, no names, nothing." Fingers poised about the keyboard, she glared at the screen. "There's gotta be something else."

Frustrated, Zoe scrolled further down the page and finally hit a link that looked promising. She clicked on it and a new page popped into view.

Dr. Soren Tepesh, Assistant Director of Eugenics in Nazi Germany. Born 1880 in Transylvania, Romania.

"Transylvania?" Zoe muttered in surprise. "What is this, some sick joke right out of Bram Stoker's novel?"

Obtained doctorate in bio-chemistry from University of Vienna, Austria. High-ranking member of Nazi Party. Early supporter of medical testing on human subjects, along with

Josef Mengele, who was often referred to as the Angel of Death. Author of several articles on life extension. Life-long advocate for creation of a "super" race of human beings. Rumored to have escaped to Argentina with a fortune in gold along with Mengele. No record for date of death. Married to Ilsse Kocher, presumed deceased in 1946.

"Holy crap! Nazis? Experiments in eugenics and a super race of people? You've got to be kidding me. Victoria's grandpa was a war criminal!"

Repulsed but intrigued, Zoe clicked on the link for Issle Tepesh.

Ilsse Tepesh, maiden name Kocher. Early member of the Nazi Party. Married to Dr. Soren Tepesh. Born 1916 in Berlin, Germany, she rose to become an SS overseer at the Auschwitz concentration camp where her husband worked. Known for her cruelty in killing prisoners to obtain their tattoos, which she turned into lamp shades and purses. Died in 1946.

"Oh, gross!" A shiver of disgust went down Zoe's back and she dug further. "Ok, so what happened to Soren?" she asked herself. "Weird. There is no record of Soren when Dragomoere shows up.

Perhaps the allies got him but then there would be some type of death certificate or obituary. There's a birth certificate for Dragomere. More weird. No picture of Soren either. Probably just some strange mix up due to the war. Wonder if Victoria knows her grandparents were Nazis?"

She brightened. "Wonder what Heath would think about all this?"

Zoe punched the print button for each of the articles, and the Wi-Fi printer on her desk whirred into action. She hoped Heath's infatuation would flame out quickly. But for his sake, if it didn't, she might have need of what she'd discovered.

'Zoe! Dinner!" The piercing voice of Zoe's mother echoed up the stairs and through the second floor.

"Is Dad home yet?" Zoe shouted back, hoping for a few more minutes on her research efforts. *I've got a start, but I could use more details, particularly about Victoria's father,* she thought, hoping this would be one of the nights her dad ran late for the family's ritual evening meal.

"You know better than that. Dinner's at six whether your father is here or not," Sally McGovern yelled back.

"Well, so much for hope of more time," Zoe groused.

The printer ground to a halt, and Zoe reluctantly set her computer aside. Sliding from her comfy place on her bed, she quickly checked herself in the mirror over her dresser before leaving the room and hurrying down the stairs and into the dining room.

"Finish setting the table," Sally instructed, passing Zoe a handful of silverware and heading back to the kitchen. "I just heard your dad pull in the driveway."

"Okay," Zoe replied.

The last utensils were barely distributed when Zoe heard the back door open. Shortly after that her father entered the room.

"Hi, sweetheart," he said, halting long enough to plant a kiss on his daughter's cheek before taking his place in the cherry-wood chair at the head of the table. "How was school today?"

"Just fine, Daddy," she assured, wondering what he'd think if she told him that the granddaughter of a former Nazi had just moved to their town.

"Super," Steve McGovern said just as Sally returned with a china plate of sliced roast beef in one hand and a matching bowl of carrots and potatoes in the other.

Steve waited for his wife to claim her chair before broaching a new subject. "I got some good news today. We've been awarded a new business consulting contract from the Powell Group, and it's a big one."

The serving spoon in Sally's hand halted in mid-air, and she looked up at her husband, a big congratulatory smile on her face. "Oh, that's great, honey," she said. "The Powell Group. Is that a new company? I don't remember hearing of them before." She spooned vegetables onto her plate and passed the bowl to Steve.

"Thanks." He then handed the bowl to Zoe before answering his wife's question. "They're new to us, but they've been around for a while. Pretty big stuff in New York circles."

Sally paused as she reached for the roast beef. "New York? What would a New York firm want with a small-town accounting firm?"

Steve shrugged. "Apparently one of their biggest clients moved to this area a couple years ago, and they've decided it would be better to work with someone local. My firm's excited about the opportunity."

"What kind of clients do they have?" Sally asked, fork poised in mid-air.

"Well, according to what I've heard, they do lots of work with financial investment firms, holding companies, and some innovative new tech companies."

Zoe's interest was peaked. "What do holding companies do, Daddy? Are they like banks? Do they loan money out for improvements or do they finance new companies?"

"Not exactly, sweetie. Powell Group is a business consulting group that's owned by a holding company. A holding company can buy any kind of business it wants to."

"Gravy or catsup?" Sally asked.

"Gravy," Steve answered, reaching for the fancy china gravy boat in Sally's hand.

Sally cut a bite of her meat and popped it in her mouth. "So, Transglobal is going to handle the local company. What's the name of the new company?" Sally asked after swallowing.

"Dragon Enterprises."

Zoe felt like someone had just punched her in the stomach.

ChAPTER
†
SIX

Heath opened the door to the Cellar Pub and was hit by the darkness of the interior and a pervasive aroma of stale beer. He could barely make out the figure of a man and woman huddled in one of the booths. They appeared to be the only customers in the place.

"Hey, kid," a rotund older man called from his place behind the bar. "Let's see some ID." He kept polishing the glass in his hand as he waited for Heath to comply.

Eyes slightly adjusted to the low light, Heath walked over to the bar, then reached into his hip pocket to pull out his wallet and show his driver's license to the bartender. The man gave one last swipe to the glass in his hand and then leaned forward so the dim light hit the small plastic-coated rectangle at a better angle.

"Twenty-one, huh? Okay." The barkeep turned and placed the glass on one of the shelves behind him before asking, "What'll it be? Beer or something harder?"

Heath shook his head. "Something softer. I'll just have a soda while I wait for my friend to arrive." He was waiting for Victoria, and the last thing he wanted to do was give her the idea that drinking in the middle of the day was normal for him.

"Suit yourself," the bartender said, scooping ice into a tall glass before using the soda gun to fill it with bubbly dark fluid.

"What do I owe you?" Heath questioned, waiting for the answer before reaching for the glass.

"Three bucks," the man replied, the red glow of a nearby neon sign reflecting on his bald head.

Heath pulled four dollar bills from his wallet and dropped them on the bar. "Thanks. I'll just pick a nice, quiet corner and wait for her."

"Who you waiting for?" the man asked as he reached for the money.

"Victoria Tepesh."

The bartender stopped before he touched the bills. Pulling his hand back, he squinted to focus more clearly on Heath, looking him up and down as he chewed on his bottom lip. "Uh, it's on the house," he finally said with a small shrug of his beefy shoulders.

Heath's hand hesitated mere inches from his glass. "How come?"

"Her father's one of our investors."

Free refreshments. Well, that at least explained why she'd picked the place when Heath asked her to meet him. Still, the location and circumstances had been a bit of a surprise to him . . . or, after some thought, maybe not. Who knew how many pies Tepesh had his fingers in? Heath hoped his upcoming talk with Victoria would shed more light on the man.

"Thanks," Heath said, reclaiming three bills and leaving a dollar tip. He picked up the glass and turned to peruse the nearly empty room, glad that happy hour didn't start for another hour according to the sign hanging near the bar's front entrance. A sound system turned low played an instrumental tune he didn't recognize as he made his way to a table near a spot-lighted pool table.

Victoria arrived before his second sip of soda. Heath stood quickly and waved her over, enjoying the sight of the woman he was attracted to approaching him with a big smile. Maybe his double-edged ploy to get better acquainted with the girl while picking up some helpful information on her father at the same time was going to work. After all, he'd always had been popular with the ladies. Zoe always teased him that it was his baby blue eyes and honey-toned skin.

"Thanks for coming," Heath said, standing and quickly pulling a chair out for her as she neared. She sat down, and he slid her chair back into place before taking his own seat again.

The bartender showed up with a tall glass of something clear and bubbly seconds after she was seated. A wedge of line hung on the rim of the glass. "There you go, Miss Tepesh. Your favorite," he said.

"Thanks, Max," Victoria replied, and the man quickly turned and returned to the bar.

Heath heard the entry door bang shut and watched two brawny guys enter and claim stools at the bar as he searched for opening words for Victoria.

"Uh, I hope I didn't screw up any plans you had." Heath began.

"No problem," she quickly assured him, concentrating on squeezing the lime into her drink. "Father's out of town, so my schedule was blank for once."

"Your dad keeps close tabs on you, huh?" Heath ventured.

Victoria nodded. "Yep. He's old fashioned. Really likes to be in control. I should be used to it by now, but I always thought he'd loosen up the reins as I got older. No such luck." She poked the mangled lime wedge into her glass and took a long drink. "Unfortunately, since he got all involved with the political stuff, he's been getting worse. Anything to do with school seems to be acceptable, but he's like a bloodhound on the prowl when it comes to guys."

Heath's heart sank. "What's the deal? He doesn't like you dating or he doesn't like some of the guys you pick?"

Victoria's bark of laughter was short and derisive. "He doesn't like *any* of the guys I pick. I was serious about him being old-fashioned. He's suddenly got some weird notion that I should marry the son of an old friend of his – some guy who lives overseas that I've never even met." She shook her head. "In this day and age. Can you believe that?"

Heath wasn't sure how to answer. Take her side or suggest her father might simply be protective of his family? He was leaning toward sympathy to show her what a nice supportive guy he could be when he had second thoughts and decided to avoid offering any opinion at all. First and foremost, he needed to concentrate on what he was there for – getting info for the interview he'd soon be asking for. That was the most important thing to remember. If he kept his eye on the prize, he should be able to glean helpful information from the man's daughter.

As much trouble as Heath and his mother had

trying to get through to Tepesh after his dad's death, he had to be sure he had a winning move before even trying to book an appointment to interview the elusive billionaire. He'd probably be smarter to slow things with Victoria way down, at least till he could tell how his plan was progressing.

More than a little frustrated, Heath suppressed a sigh.

"So what is it you wanted to talk with me about?" Victoria asked, stirring her drink with a straw.

Heath downed a hurried slug of soda as he searched for an acceptable reason for his invitation. "Well . . . uh, since you're new around here, I thought I'd see if you had any questions about the group. And I, uh, I wanted to get your opinion on a possible location for the meetings as well as your take on scheduling." He winced at his answer to her question, wondering if it sounded as lame to her as it did to him.

"What do you have in mind?"

"Well, what times do you think might be best? Right after school or a little later in the evening?" Heath offered, wondering if he might eventually be able to finagle getting together for a quick burger before one of the meetings.

Victoria shot that idea down quickly. "Definitely right after school. That way I can tell my father it's a school-related meeting."

"Oh. Uh, okay."

"Have you got a particular place in mind?" Victoria asked.

"Yeah, I do. Just Beans. The one here and not in Madison," Heath answered, grateful that he'd actually done some preliminary scouting. "It's a coffee shop located near the school, which would be really convenient. Any student who joins the group probably knows where it is, and it's got a private room that they sometimes use for birthday parties and events like that. A nice-sized room in the back where we'll have the privacy the professor wants. We were lucky. Turns out the owner's a friend of Stein's. The professor wrote an article about him several years ago and they've been friends ever since. He says it's ours if we want it."

Ice clicked as Victoria gave her drink another quick swirl with her straw before replying. "That's not one of Father's investments, so it sounds absolutely perfect to me."

"Good to know," Heath replied.

Victoria finished off the last of her drink, gathered her purse, and pushed to her feet.

"Sorry to run but I need to head for home. Father's out of town, but my mother will be expecting me." She sighed. "*And* my brother, who's almost as bad as my father . . ."

Heath clamored upward. "Uh, sure. I still have

stuff to do, too. I'll walk you out." *Well, mission accomplished. Sorta,* he thought as he followed her to the door.

He barely noticed that, a few steps behind him, one of the men at the bar bent to whisper something to his companion. Then both of them pushed their barely tasted drinks away and bid good-bye to the bartender before heading to the exit. The biggest guy caught the door Heath had held open for Victoria just before it swung closed.

CHAPTER
†
SEVEN

The first official meeting of Stein's new organization was held at Just Beans in the late afternoon the next week. Heath had gone along with Victoria's five o'clock suggestion so she could pass it off as a school-related event. He justified the choice by assuring himself that other possible recruits to the group might have a similar problem.

Heath showed up early to make sure the pleasant room was set up just right. Zoe arrived a few minutes later. She dropped her oversized purse on the table beside Heath's book bag and hurried to help him move some of the tables, so they were lined up facing the slightly larger table he'd already placed at the front of the room for Professor Stein's use.

Hands on her jean-clad hips, Zoe surveyed the

room, turning to take in the cheery, pale-yellow walls and the large chalkboard hung behind the biggest table. "I didn't know this room was even here," she declared. "Did you have any trouble convincing the owner to let us use it?"

"Nope," Heath answered. "Turns out the owner's a former Marine who knows Stein from way back, when the professor was doing a series of stories on military heros."

"Lucky for us," Zoe said with a nod. "This is going to be perfect. Good choice, Heath."

"Thanks," he replied as two young men poked their head in the door, spotted him, and entered.

Heath introduced Zoe to the most recent additions he'd found for the group. Chuck and Robert, both political science majors, had snapped at the chance to join when Heath approached them in the class they shared.

"We're waiting for Professor Stein," Heath explained. "Help yourselves to something to drink while we wait on the others." He nodded toward a table at the back of the room where Carter King, owner of the establishment, had set up a coffee pot and cups, plus bowls of ice for the pitchers of soft drinks and water scattered on the tabletop.

Professor Stein had stopped Heath before he left the journalism class that morning to tell him he'd come up with a rough agenda for that night's meeting. He planned to explain the group's goals to the attendees and then lead the evening's discussion. Heath was psyched. Things were finally on a roll.

Zoe, Heath, and the two new guys were filling the waiting time with small talk when David arrived a few minutes later, followed almost immediately by Professor Stein.

"We're at the middle table," Zoe called. A quick survey of the room sent David straight for the table topped with Zoe's favorite purse side-by-side with Heath's familiar backpack. David detoured to drop off his own backpack and an old-fashioned steno tablet before pulling up an empty chair for the table, and then joining his friends at the beverage station.

Professor Stein arrived, going straight to the big table at the front where he stacked a bundle of stapled printed pages and several small boxes before joining the others. Approaching the group, he glanced at his watch and asked, "We about ready?"

Heath's gaze flickered to the doorway and back to the professor. "Should be one more," he replied, wondering if Victoria wasn't going to show or if late arrival was simply habitual with her – or maybe her father had other plans for her that evening. Heath wondered if he was foolish to consider trying to juggle a personal friendship with the pretty newcomer *and* at the same time mine that relationship for information about her father.

He mulled over the disturbing question. Would

spending time with Victoria gain him enough information to create viable questions for use during the interview he hoped would open a door for him? On the personal side, Victoria was a knock-out and he'd felt attraction even before he learned who she was – but again he wondered if he shouldn't be concentrating on the important stuff first.

Their talk at the Cellar Pub had provided a little more insight into the Tepesh family, but it hadn't furthered his hoped-for relationship with the girl *or* provided that essential key for getting an interview appointment with her dad when the time was right. Disappointed at his lack of progress on the personal side but realizing that might go down in flames anyway if Victoria found out what he was up to, Heath decided he had to concentrate his thoughts only on the hoped-for interview with the president of Dragon Enterprises. First things first, and that meant developing that strong list of questions – some to maintain his cover and some to start scratching away at what Heath believed had been a cover-up about his father's death.

Victoria was the last to arrive. When Zoe stilled and looked away from the door, Heath wondered about her sudden change of demeanor, then pushed the worry from his mind to nod in greeting as Victoria took a scat at the second table over. She smiled at him – a nice smile, but not the kind he would expect from a girl who had any personal interest in him. *Oh, well, can't win them all,* Heath thought, lifting his hand to deliver a little wave and hoping that his possible conduit to Tepesh was still intact.

A few minutes later Professor Stein tapped a spoon against the side of his coffee cup, bringing the small group to attention. "Welcome," he said with a smile, walking to the empty area in front of the table serving as his make-shift desk. "I'm delighted to have you all here for this first meeting. We may be starting small, but with time I hope to see our little organization expand in size. I believe we're going to need an army to combat the trouble that's brewing in our world."

Stein scanned the room. Apparently satisfied, he continued. "Before we get down to our first discussion, I think it's necessary to pay a little homage to some brave folks who battled evil back in World War II."

Stein turned to his table and picked up one of the small boxes, holding it up and giving it a shake that resulted in a metallic rattle as he slowly paced the open area in front of his table. "Legend has it that an organization of Dutch resistance fighters found a safe way to identify each other in times when a slip in security could cost a life. The resistance members wore blue paperclips on the collars of their shirts so they could recognize each other without saying a word or giving some fancy signal that the enemy might eventually recognize."

Heath, Zoe, and David exchanged looks that clearly revealed that they wanted to know more. Stein obliged.

The professor moved forward, handing the box to Heath. "Help yourself to a handful of these paperclips. Get enough that you'll always have some for yourself. Keep the extras to pass out to anyone you believe will be a good addition to our group."

Heath opened the box and took out half-a-dozen of the bright blue paperclips before passing the box to Zoe.

Zoe extracted her handful and passed the box on to David. The little box continued to move from one student to another. Each one took a small handful of paperclips before passing the box to the next person in line. The last student retrieved his clips then slipped from his chair and placed the almost empty box back on Stein's table.

Stein nodded approval. "Get in the habit of always sliding one over the neckline of your tee-shirt or near the wing-tip of your collar or even on the top of a pocket. Just make sure it's visible to anyone who might be looking for it."

Each student obediently slid a paperclip into place on his or her clothing and then deposited the rest into a pocket or purse.

"Good," Professor Stein said. "Now, let's get down to the reason we're here. After all my years in the news business, I've come to believe that we're about to come up against something as evil as what those people faced in World War II. Dark forces are gathering, and certain things I've heard make me believe that their goal is to take over our government, our country."

The students exchanged looks of confusion tinged with interest and a hint of fear.

Stein began to slowly pace. "I want everyone to be careful, to take no chances. We're going to work slowly, carefully. These people won't fight nice if they figure out what we're doing. Keep in mind that we have a perfect cover story, so we really shouldn't raise any attention. As far as the world will know, we're an educational organization, interested in discussing civic and ethical issues – and that's all they need to know." Stein halted and raised a finger in the air. "But we have a plan they don't know about. While most of us do research and keep our ears to the ground, the journalism majors in our group will set up interviews with rich and powerful people in our community. Those interviews should help us find out where those people stand on vital issues, who we can trust, and who is working against the values of this country."

The room was almost eerily quiet as the students held their breaths and waited for the professor to continue.

"If we're convinced that some haven't gone to the dark side . . ." Stein began. "If we believe we can trust them, believe that they believe as we do, then they might be recruited to join our organization, but only if we're sure they're trust-worthy and not afraid to stay the course, whatever that may be. Other interviews will be used to ascertain if a person has thrown in with those who are intent on gaining enough power to run the world and drain it of its profits and resources for their own benefit. In other words, they'll be identifying the enemies of our country and all it stands for."

Heath stole a quick glance at Victoria. Would she put two and two together and figure out that much of his interest was because of her father? If she caught on to what he had in mind and figured out her father might wind up on the "enemy side" of the situation, all bets might be off. Chances were she'd never give him an opportunity to get better acquainted and she might even warn her father not to do any interviews with him or anybody else in the class.

Heath gave a sigh of acceptance. Solving the mystery of what had really happened to his father was more important than anything. He shook the misgivings from his mind and turned his full attention on the professor.

Stein stilled and searched the face of each student as if trying to see into their minds. Finally, he nodded and said, "And when we find those people, we'll do our best to expose their evil plans."

"Wow," Heath muttered under his breath, the hopelessness he'd felt since his father's death slowly slipping away.

CHAPTER
†
EIGHT

By the third meeting they had over three dozen people in attendance. Even Carter King was dropping in quite often to listen to the discussions when business out front was light. All participants wore a small blue paperclip on their clothing, unnoticeable by all but those in the know.

Professor Stein settled his followers down and began the evening's lecture. "I'm sure you're all familiar with our governor and the many questions about how he mysteriously won in spite of the overwhelming odds against him. Rumor has it that he threw huge amounts of money into the race, but no one knows where that money came from. I've done a little digging, and it sure looks like there was a link between him and some awfully powerful finance guys."

A murmur rippled through the audience. Carter, who had claimed his usual chair near the entrance in case the front-of-the-store employees got busy and needed his help, spoke up. "I've got some just-breaking news for you, Jack. One of my network guys just told me that Walters announced his candidacy this afternoon. He's officially thrown his hat in the ring for this year's presidential race. Dead Crow's own billionaire, Dragomere Tepesh, is rumored to be the head of Walters' campaign committee."

The look on Professor Stein's face left no question as to how disturbed he was to hear that news.

"To top it off, he reportedly has the backing of many more of the country's billionaires." Carter continued. "Unfortunately, there's no direct evidence, but I've heard that the Citizens United decision made it easier for billionaires to buy politicians who were all too happy to be bought."

Stein speared his friend with a concerned look. "Well, that certainly puts a different spin on our schedule. The election is only months away. We've got a lot to accomplish. Guess we'll have to ramp up our timeline."

Heath watched the professor peruse the room, noting that he was careful not to let his gaze linger on Victoria as he asked, "Anyone else heard any-thing about this announcement?"

Victoria sat very still for a long moment, then she slowly raised her hand.

Stein looked pleased. "You have information you'd like to share, Miss Tepesh?" he questioned.

"I . . . uh, a few days ago I might have heard something that could be helpful. It's not much, but maybe–"

"Excellent," Stein replied with an eager nod. "Every little bit of information we can gather could help."

"Well, I'm not positive, of course, but I did overhear my father and my brother talking about Governor Walters and a list they'd compiled. I think they were discussing who might be willing to con-tribute to his campaign."

An older woman sitting at the second row of tables frowned. "Tepesh? Is that the guy who funds several orphanages?"

"He does, but I haven't heard much about them recently," Victoria said with a shrug. "It's not unusual for Father to be interested in some enterprise for a short time and then sell out if it's not as profitable as he'd hoped."

The woman who'd asked the question frowned. "Profitable? How could anyone make money run-ning an orphanage?"

Victoria shook her head. "I, uh, I really don't

know. My father and my brother handle the family's businesses."

"That list you spoke of, Miss Tepesh . . ." Stein intervened. "Do you happen to remember any of the names?"

Victoria nodded. "Uh, yeah, some of them. They were mostly friends of the family, all very wealthy, and some very successful businessmen."

"Do you think you could write down the names for me?" the professor asked.

"Well, sure, I guess," Victoria replied. "Father put the list in his study desk. If I can't remember, I guess I can make a copy of it."

Wow, thought Heath. *She must still be really ticked at her father if she's willing to do that. Maybe my hopes of her helping me get an interview appointment with him aren't just pie in the sky.*

"Sounds like we're dealing with one of those best-selling fiction novels," one of the students said with a grin. "I know politics can be dirty, but you don't really think there are secret groups working to influence the next presidential election, do you?"

"I'm afraid this isn't fiction," Stein answered. "I believe we're up against some-thing very dangerous, and I think we've got to explore everything we can. For instance, there've been rumors for several years of an organization of multi-national corporations whose goal is to make a profit no matter what they have to do or who they might hurt. Money is their god. And, from what I've heard, the greedy bastards are willing to cross any line as long as they can fill their bank accounts."

David shook his head in stunned amazement. "Corporations manipulating events and contributions for a national election? That sounds more like it's a high stakes chess game, what with all the manipulation and maneuvering that would take. Someone doing that would have to believe they had a chance to gain control of the whole state."

"Personally, I'm worried far more that their goal is domination of the whole country," Stein remarked.

"But is that even possible?" another student asked.

Carter stood and walked to the front of the room. "I heard from another ol' military buddy not long ago. We saw combat together and now he's got some important job at the Pentagon," he explained. He cast an inquisitive look in Stein's direction.

"You've got the floor, Carter," the professor said. "Please continue."

Carter nodded. "My friend claims there's a Wall Street group that already controls most of the elected offices of this state." The former Marine shook his head as if to deny even the thought of such a diabolical situation. "According to my friend, their goal is to buy up the state facilities and utilities for pennies. Once they're in control, they can raise rates all they want to. And that's not all. He says they're already working to push through other legislation that will effectively wipe out the middle class, leaving the rich in charge and the lower class left with not much more than hard work in low paying jobs, which makes them virtual slaves to the wealthy."

A new wave of murmurs rippled through the room.

"Now what? If all these rumors should prove true, is there anything at all we can do to stop those people from accomplishing their goals?" Zoe asked, the tone of her voice betraying her worry.

Stein paused, a frown on his face as he contemplated Zoe's question. "Well, I can think of at least a couple of things we can do while we try to ferret out the truth of what's going on. Those of you from the journalism class can get started on your interviews if your choice has been approved. If you haven't made a choice yet, then you can do some more research to see if you can find a candidate that interests you."

"What about those of us who aren't in your class?" someone asked.

"There's an important job for the rest of you to tackle," Stein answered. "You can keep an eye out for other people who'd fit in with our little group. Just be careful. We don't want word of what we're looking into getting out, so be very cautious about who you approach and how much you share as you look for new recruits. But keep looking. Something tells me we're going to need all the help we can get."

CHAPTER
†
NINE

Heath and his friends left the meeting energized by the evening's conversation and perplexed about what their small group might do about it except concentrate on their interviews.

"Hey, Heath, if you need tech support or anything for your interview, you know who to call," David reminded.

"Thanks. I've got a couple of things in mind that I'll need your help on," Heath replied, casting a sideways glance at Victoria, who seemed to be growing anxious as she searched her expensive hobo purse for her car keys. "We can compare notes once I've got the interview booked. Say, anyone up for a stop at BeBe's Burgers before we head for home? I wouldn't mind some feedback on this upcoming interview thing."

"Oh, I can't," Victoria replied, still rummaging in her purse. "This meeting ran later than usual. Father will flip if I don't get home soon."

Heath tried to hide his disappointment. He'd hoped he might be able to lay some groundwork for his interview request. "Okay. See you tomorrow."

"Sure. See you in class," Victoria replied, finally retrieving her keys. "Night, all." She smiled and nodded, then quickly crossed to the first row of parked cars.

"You think she'll come through for you on that interview?" David asked as they all watched Victoria climb in her shiny Mercedes and pull out of the parking lot at high speed.

Heath shrugged. "Who knows? I can't help but have some doubts, but after what she said in the meeting – telling us about the list of donors and volunteering out of the blue to somehow get that list for the professor – wouldn't you think she'd be willing to help me get an appointment for an interview?"

"Well, we can always hope," David said, stuffing his steno pad in his backpack before slinging a strap over one shoulder. "Sorry, I'm out on the interview planning for tonight. Gotta study for a test tomorrow."

He hugged Zoe good-bye and planted a playful punch on Heath's bicep before heading to his vehicle. "Hang in there, buddy," he called back to Heath. "I'm bettin' Victoria will come through with that introduction to her father. How could she say no to a stud like you?"

Heat climbed Heath's face. He shot Zoe an embarrassed glance. "Huh, guess it's just you and me then? You still interested?"

Zoe looped her arm through his. "Absolutely," she said with a firm nod.

§

Fifteen minutes later Heath and Zoe were seated across from each other in BeBe's back booth. Scattered speakers played a popular rock tune, barely audible over the babble of the crowded dining area. A harried waitress took their order – coffee for Heath, a vanilla shake for Zoe, and a large order of chili cheese fries for them to share.

"So tell me what you've come up with so far," Zoe said as soon as the waitress hurried away.

Heath pulled a folded sheet of notebook paper from his pocket, unfolded it, and spread it out on the table before retrieving the ballpoint pen that had resided beside it. "Well, to begin with, I thought I'd ask him about his background, how he got started in business, that kind of thing," Heath said, the pen hovering at-the-ready over the paper. "You know, kinda break the ice."

Zoe paused, her mouth pinched in concentration as she seemed to contemplate his answer and what she might add to it. "Humm. Just a thought," she finally offered. "Have you considered doing any earlier background research on him before the interview? You might be able to get down to the meat of your questions quicker if you already had some of that preliminary information."

"You're good, girl," Heath said with a grin. "I got so tied up in getting the interview and trying to figure out how to get to the questions about my father that I didn't pay enough attention to the simple things I could do beforehand."

Zoe shrugged away the compliment. "I think it might be worth the effort. There's so much personal stuff on the Internet now, you might find out all sorts of interesting things about their family history."

Heath nodded in agreement. "Great idea, Zoe. Thanks. I'll do that."

She gave another little shrug of her shoulders. "Who knows? Maybe he inherited family money and that funded his first business, whatever that was."

"Right. It'd be interesting to find out just what kind of business he started in, how many pies he's got his fingers in now. Like that orphan thing the lady mentioned. That's kinda weird, don't you think?"

"Yes, I do."

"Well, anything I find out is bound to be helpful. There might at least be a list of all his businesses, what they manufacture, where they are," Heath continued, remembering how often he and his mother had been told after his father's death that Tepesh was out of town at another of his companies. "Although that might be something I can ask Victoria about, don't you think?"

Frowning, Zoe swirled her straw in her thick shake for a long moment before lifting it and licking away a clot of ice cream. "I'm sure you can," she finally answered.

Heath was still scribbling notes on the paper when the waitress arrived with their appetizer. He finished his last entry and pushed his paper and pen aside to make room for the plate of steaming fries.

"Anything else come to mind?" he asked as he unwrapped his silverware, picked up his fork and speared several fries from the gooey pile. He chewed, swallowed, and speared again, not even noticing Zoe's hesitation as she quickly turned her attention to unrolling her own napkin to fumble for her utensils.

"You're gonna do fine," she assured him.

"Damn, I hope so," Heath said, another fry-laden forkful poised in mid-air. "I thought this would be so straight-forward, so easy, and now . . .

now I just don't know. After listening to Professor Stein tonight, I realize there might be more at stake here than I ever imagined. What if Victoria says no to my request for help when it gets right down to the nitty-gritty?"

Zoe's dark eyes searched Heath's worried face for a long moment, then she reached across the table and placed her hand on his. "It's going to be okay, Heath. You're a great guy, a straight-arrow guy. Victoria's going to see that. However you decide to handle this, your plan will work, so just bite the bullet and ask."

A grateful smile quirked the corner of Heath's mouth. He turned his hand over, gripped hers, and gave it a squeeze. "Thanks, Zoe. You're the best. I can always count on you."

"Yes, you can, Heath," Zoe said, her answering smile tender and a little tremulous. "Yes, you can."

CHAPTER

†

TEN

Zoe was delighted when Heath called her the very next night. "I did it, Zoe!" he bragged. "I just screwed up my nerve and called Victoria to ask her to help me get an appointment with her dad. And she said yes!"

Zoe's grip on her cell phone tightened as she tried not to show her disappointment that the call was association-related not personal. She managed a weak laugh and assured her friend that his news was wonderful.

"That's not the most amazing part of it, Zoe. She said she'd ask him, and then she called me back practically immediately and said her father's going out of town first thing in the morning so he's gonna work me in for the interview tonight."

"Tonight?" Zoe repeated, cold chills trailing down her back. "You mean *this* night?"

"Yep, I'm supposed to be there in thirty minutes."

"It's awfully late. Don't you think it would be better to wait and see if she really brings in that list for Stein? Maybe you should book it for a couple days later, when you can do it earlier in the evening, when you'd be fresher."

"Nope. I'll be fine," Heath assured her.

"But . . . uh, are you sure you're prepared? What about the Internet research we talked about . . . you did get that done, didn't you?"

"No, I didn't have time to do any, but don't worry. I've got my notes from last night, and I'm sure I can handle it."

Cell held in a death grip against her ear, Zoe dropped her head into her free hand, rubbing her forehead in hopes of chasing away the beginning of a pounding headache.

Damn, damn, damn! I should have told him about the Internet entries straight out last night. I screwed up big time, giving him hints of where to look and thinking he'd realize something was way off with that family, off enough that he'd figure out that he should be very careful in any dealings with any of them. Off enough that he might realize Victoria is not the girl he needs in his life.

"Seriously, Heath, I think it might be better if

you waited till you were better prepared," Zoe said, hoping he'd come to his senses and listen to her. She searched her mind for anything else she could say that might make him change his mind, but her brain just kept playing the same ol' song: *I screwed up the whole deal. I should have told him what kind of people he was going to be dealing with. I should have told him.*

Heath snorted his dismissal of postponement. "No. The timing couldn't be better. It'll be great to have this over with. Stein will be happy if I pick up some clues about Tepesh's involvement with the governor. And Victoria says her dad is in a great mood and eager to do the interview. I'm already on my way. Don't worry, I've got everything covered. David's gonna meet me half-way. He's got some fancy memory card or something to put in my phone so I can record the meeting even if it's a long one. I couldn't ask for things to work out any better. Really."

"Wait, Heath," Zoe pleaded. "There's something important I need to–"

"There's David. Gotta go. I'll call you when I'm done."

"–tell you." Zoe's unheard words echoed in the hollow silence of their severed connection.

§

Heath let out a low whistle as he neared Tepesh's sprawling property. A tall black wrought-iron fence surrounded the grounds, backed by a thick privet hedge. He turned off the road and onto a short driveway which quickly ended at a huge closed gate and a fancy guard shack. Heath could see a winding drive on the other side of the gate, glimpses of vast expanses of lush grass, and the shadowed shape of an immense house at the top of a hill.

A burly man in a tailored black security uniform stepped out of the little gabled building. Tall and very muscular, his hand hovered near the butt of his holstered gun. "Your name, sir?"

"Heath Harkness," he answered. "Mr. Tepesh is expecting me." I'm, uh . . . I'm a friend of Victoria's," he added, hoping that would make the man stop looking at him like he was some sort of invader.

The guard nodded, but his eyes remained dark and cold. "You're expected," the man said. "Follow the drive up and park on the parking area just past the house. Leave your keys in the car."

"Sure," Heath said with a forced smile.

The guard's face remained frozen. He simply executed an about-face and returned to his shack. A few seconds later the mammoth gate began to slowly swing open. Heath drove through, glad to escape the man's disquieting gaze.

The meandering drive led him past broad sweeps of manicured lawn on each side. As he neared the house in the dim light provided by the setting sun, he spotted another guard garbed in the same black uniform as the guy at the gate. To Heath's surprise, the man carried a rifle as well as the gun on his hip. Two sweeping curves later, Heath caught a glimpse of another guard, also in matching uniform and armed with a rifle, patrolling the perimeter of the biggest house he'd ever seen.

He'd expected fancy but nothing like this. He calculated the square foot measurement to be close to forty thousand. "House, my ass. This thing's a damn mansion! I guess that explains all the guards. Ol' Tepesh must be afraid the masses might want to take some of his goodies," Heath muttered to himself as he pulled into the half-circle parking area, which held several expensive vehicles and turned off his engine.

Glancing around and seeing no one, he took a moment to carefully pull his cell phone from his pants pocket. Making sure he held it well below the sight-line of the car's windows, he punched the record icon then slipped the phone back in the pocket. Grabbing one last glance in the rearview mirror to check that every hair was in place, he exited his vehicle.

It took several minutes for Heath to walk to the front steps of the house and climb them. The echo of his footsteps followed him across the broad front porch. In front of an ornately carved door, he paused, took a deep breath, and pushed the elaborate doorbell button. There was a muted ring, then mere seconds later the huge wooden door swung open.

"Good evening, sir," a tall, thin man in full formal dress greeted in solemn tones. "How may I help you?"

Heath gazed at the portion of the foyer he could see and realized that room alone was bigger than the house he and his mom lived in. Giving himself a mental shake, he hurried to answer the question. "Uh, Mr. Tepesh is expecting me. I'm Victoria's friend."

The butler gave him a cool-eyed once-over, then slowly dipped his head.

Might as well give up the name dropping, Heath thought. *It apparently doesn't impress anyone, not even the hired help.*

"Ah, yes. Please enter, sir, and follow me. Mr. Tepesh is just finishing up a meeting. He'll be with you shortly."

Heath's jaw dropped as he followed the butler through the marble-floored entry then down a hallway twice as large as any of the rooms in his house. When they reached a set of double doors, the man paused to swing them open and motion Heath inside.

"Please make yourself comfortable in the study, sir, and help yourself to some refreshment. You'll find a full bar on the right side, near the patio door. There's a particularly nice twelve-year bourbon you might like to try, the one with the red label. Or I can have tea or coffee brought, if you prefer."

For a moment, Heath teetered between worrying that it wouldn't be appropriate for him to imbibe while on a professional call and wondering if they might be treating him as a welcome guest because of his connection with Victoria. Guest status won out. "Thank you, I believe I will," he said, hopeful he was doing the right thing.

"Excellent." The man bobbed his head in acknowledgement and waited for Heath to enter the room before he pulled the door shut so quietly that Heath had to turn and look to confirm that he was gone.

Heath stuck his hands in his pockets and did his best to look at ease as he moved further into a room that looked unlike any he'd ever seen before.

"Wow," he murmured as he slowly wandered the perimeter.

A fireplace graced one wall. Half a dozen black leather club chairs sat three to each side in front of the gigantic stone structure. Greek statues on pedestals peppered the room. An abundance of built-in bookcases held volumes of every shape and size, many bound in forest green leather with gold-stamped titles in foreign languages on their spines.

A mammoth desk dominated the far corner, angled so its user could look out at a patio barely visible now that night shadows had crept over it. A small glass cabinet sitting nearby held even more books, the volumes looking eons old.

As a final flourish, the paneled walls were hung with the stuffed heads of exotic animals – a black-maned lion, a fierce tiger, a trio of snarling wolves, and a grizzly bear, long sharp teeth bared. The creatures' glassy-eyed stares seemed to follow Heath as he moved about the room. A frisson of discomfort skittered through him, and he turned and headed straight for the bar.

The red-labeled bottle sat center, upfront. Heath grabbed a crystal highball glass and poured a shot he hoped would calm his nerves. The mellow liquor went down like silk, easing the knot in the pit of his stomach.

"Ah, better," Heath murmured to himself. Then, hearing very dim voices from the hall, he quickly swallowed the rest of the liquor and sat the glass back on the bar. He turned just as the door swung open and a tall, dark man he assumed was Dragomere Tepesh entered the room.

A flicker of movement behind his probable host caught Heath's attention and he glimpsed a slim, dark-haired man hurrying in the direction of the front door. *Is that . . . ? Yes. Yes, it is. That's Governor*

Walters! Heath thought, his mind whirling as he realized he'd confirmed one of Stein's suspicions without having to ask a single question.

Tepesh stopped and studied Heath before he finally spoke. "Mr. Harkness, I presume. I have several important tasks to take care of when we're through, so let's get on with the interview, shall we," the man said, his words more command than question.

"Of course." Hand extended, Heath hurried forward. "I want to thank you for this opportunity."

Heath's offered hand was ignored as Tepesh pivoted and made his own stop at the bar where he selected a fancy wine decanter and poured himself a drink. Stemmed wine glass in hand, he turned and moved toward the closest row of club chairs.

"Help yourself to another drink, if you'd like," he told Heath, "then have a seat."

How'd he know I had a drink? Heath wondered, resisting the urge to scan the room for evidence of a security camera. He shook off his suspicions, assuring himself that he was being ridiculous, that Tepesh must have noticed his now out-of-place glass where he'd set it on the rim of the bar. "I'm fine, sir. Thank you," he said, hurrying toward the seating area.

For a moment he considered choosing a chair across from Victoria's father so he could watch his face, but at the last second, Heath swerved and claimed the chair next to his subject, hoping that the special recording card in his cell phone would work better if they were closer.

Tepesh raised his glass and took a sip, savoring the taste of the dark red liquid before he swallowed and said, "Proceed with your questions."

"I, uh, I couldn't help but notice you have a slight accent," Heath began, not wishing to jump into the heavy issues right off the bat.

"I lived abroad when I was a child. I suppose I picked up a little accent then. My parents liked to travel internationally and we moved frequently," Tepesh explained. Then up went his glass and he took another swallow before balancing his drink on the arm of his chair while he sat silent for a long moment. Finally, he spoke again. "I understand you're a classmate of my daughter's."

Heath nodded. "Uh, yes, I am," he answered. He blinked and hesitated, slightly irritated that his mind was beginning to feel muddled. *Should have skipped the bourbon,* he thought. *Damn stuff must have been high proof.*

"I assume you have more questions?" Tepesh prodded.

"Well, yes, of course. No article would be complete without information on your businesses, how you got started . . ." *What else?* Heath probed his brain, beginning to worry because the fuzzy feeling in his head was intensifying. "Your, uh, your current project – that chemical product rumor says your company is working on."

Tepesh shook his head. "Not chemicals," he said, a hint of disdain in his voice. "Pharmaceuticals for the good of mankind. Formulas that will provide amazing benefits, such as stronger, more invincible bodies, sharper minds. But, enough said. It's too soon to divulge details of the project. There're all those patents and licenses and intellectual content issues to deal with first. I'm sure you understand about that."

"Of course, but . . ." Heath gave his head a shake. The questions he'd so carefully planned were in his mind, but getting them out was fast becoming impossible. Something was very wrong. He was suddenly overcome with the thought that he needed to get to the one issue that mattered most to him. This might be his only chance to find out what really happened to his father.

"Dragon Enterprises," Heath said, pushing the words out through the thickening fog in his brain. "My father . . . my father died in an accident there–"

"Ah, yes. Unfortunate," Tepesh remarked. "I remember quite well. And how is your dear mother doing? Too bad she had to go back to full-time work at that restaurant. What was the name? Delilah's Diner? Yes, that was it."

Heath blinked in surprise. *What? The man couldn't take a phone call from us back then, but now he knows where Mom works? What the hell?*

A flicker of movement across the room caught Heath's attention. The entry door had just opened and a young man with a shaved head and the same strong features as his host was ambling in. Heath shook his head again, hoping to clear away the cobwebs.

"This the guy who's been pestering Victoria?" the younger man asked.

"One and the same," Tepesh replied.

"Did you tell him she's promised to someone else? That she'll be headed for the Old Country at Christmas break?"

"Why bother, Gregor?" Tepesh said with a dismissive shrug. "The issue is being taken care of."

Gregor? The name rang a bell. A niggling memory surfaced in Heath's befuddled brain. Of course. Victoria's brother. Why was he there? He wasn't supposed to be part of the interview.

Gregor gave a snort. "About time," he told his father. "Well, at least we have plenty of time to find out what this guy's really up to."

Tepesh waved away his son's comment. "Never mind about that. I'm well aware of the situation. I already have the perfect solution."

A frown slid across Gregor's face. "But what

about this kid's connection with that damn reporter who's been digging into the upcoming election situation for months."

Tepesh's dark eyes narrowed. "I have reasons for doing things my way. We've whipped the citizens of this state into an appropriate frenzy and they're ripe for change at any cost. We must take advantage of this opportunity while we can. We've made great progress in recruiting supporters, from upper echelon officers in the local police force to state-wide political figures. A couple special groups will be attending the next rally. TV coverage will be exceptional. And the funding is rolling in from those who see the future of this state, this country, as we do. The wealth of the world will be ours if we stick to the plan."

"Yeah, but–"

Face a tight mask of controlled anger, Tepesh leaned forward. "Do not question me again. Our most important challenge is making sure Walters is elected President. The new voting software must be tested and the final version put in place. To do so requires an unbelievably tight schedule that we *must* adhere to. Nothing else matters right now." The deadly quiet tone of his voice clearly indicated that the subject was closed.

Wealth? Walters? Police officers? Voting soft-ware? The words Tepesh had spoken whirled in

Heath's brain. He tried to make sense of the conversation blithely taking place as if his presence no longer mattered, but aside from a few key words, his muddled mind was having little luck deciphering their discussion.

"But what about Victoria and—" Gregor insisted.

"Silence!" Tepesh demanded. "You heard what I said. We do it my way."

Gregor quickly shut up, his mouth tight and thin.

A garbled thought plucked at Heath's mind. *Control . . . gotta . . . get it back.* Fluttery hands gripping the arms of his chair, he slid forward and tried to stand up. His legs didn't seem to want to cooperate and he fell back in his chair. Worry overtook his initial surprise. "Wh-What's going on?" he asked, his words slurred.

Tepesh ignored the question. "Summon Reilly and Smith. It's time to get this over with," he instructed Gregor before leaning back in his chair and taking another leisurely sip of his wine.

Heath's thoughts were a windstorm of confusion. He could hear and see, but little made sense, and his body seemed to have a will of its own. He watched as Gregor left the room and returned shortly with two big, brawny men. One had a dark buzz cut, and the other, bulkier and taller than his partner, had slicked his thinning hair back and close to his scalp. Their black uniforms hugged bodies bulging with muscles. He squinted up at the men. One looked a little familiar although for the life of him he couldn't figure out why.

"You know what to do, Mr. Smith?" Tepesh said.

"Yes, sir," the man with the buzz cut responded.

"And Mr. Reilly, you checked the route?"

The taller man nodded. "Yes, sir. We're ready."

"Excellent. Our guest may need a little help getting up."

"Yes, sir," the men said, moving quickly to the side of Heath's chair. Each gripped one of his arms and then pulled him upward and out of his seat.

Head bobbing like a drunken Jack-in-the-Box, Heath barely managed to get his feet under him as they stood him up. He tried to pull away from the men and was shocked when his mind's command and his body's response didn't connect at all. Feeling the first frissons of real fear, his mind grappled with a flood of questions. *What's happening? Where's Victoria?* And the most disturbing thought of all: *Oh, god, did she set me up somehow?*

That thought fueled another feeble attempt to free himself, all to no avail. He was at their mercy.

Supported by the surprisingly powerful guards, Heath was propelled out of the room, into the hallway, and then to the foyer, his feet managing only an occasional shuffle-step as the men roughly dragged him to the front door where the butler politely opened the door and watched quietly as the guards manhandled Heath across the porch.

Once down the front stairs, Heath was shoved into the backseat of a black limo parked at the curb. The men pulled and prodded until he was settled enough that they could close the car's rear door. Heath slumped against the corner formed by seat and door, his head leaning against the tinted glass of the limo's side window as the men quickly opened the front doors and slipped into their places, Smith behind the wheel, Reilly in the passenger seat.

The engine purred to life, rousing Heath from his strange lethargy. "Car . . . my car," he weakly protested.

"Don't worry," the driver said, throwing a quick glance over his shoulder. "We'll take care of it."

"Where . . . where are we going?" Heath managed in slurred words.

Wide smile plastered on his face, Reilly turned and gave Heath a wink. "Home, brother. You're going home."

Heath was still trying to make sense of the man's words when the car accelerated, the soft purr of the motor obliterated by the raucous laughter coming from the front seats.

The limo wound its way down the long drive to the gate. When the guard stepped out of the shack, the driver blinked his lights twice, earning an informal two-finger salute. The guard returned to his fancy shack and the big gate opened.

The car exited, hooked a right-hand turn, and was soon gliding over the back roads of Waukesha County. Slumped in his corner, head still against the window glass, Heath watched the shadowy side-of-the-road landscape flow past, the huge silver moon hanging low in the sky highlighting shrubs and trees and swatches of earth peppered in wild grass that swayed in a slight wind.

Heath had no concept of time, but he felt a flash of relief when he spotted a familiar landmark – a roadside sign advertising *"Green Shores Development Coming Soon"* – and his fuzzy mind remembered that the road they were on would eventually lead to his neighborhood.

Relief blossomed. Home was not too far away. Every time they passed a recognizable landmark, Heath felt a little more at ease.

Making himself a silent promise to stay away from bourbon from then on, Heath closed his eyes momentarily. All he wanted to do now was climb into his bed and sleep off the wooziness that still filled his head.

The car topped a low hill and made a sharp right-hand turn and Heath's eyes snapped open.

That's not right, he thought. Squinting through his window he could see the dark silhouette of a tall metal fence amongst the scattered clumps of trees that kept hurtling past his window.

The sedan made a slow S-curve, revealing the hulk of a three-story building behind the fence. Flickers of light pierced the shadows – windows that glowed like watchful golden eyes in the dark. Heath struggled for comprehension. *Where are we?*

An elaborate arched sign over the gated entry in the fence gave him the answer. *Dragon Enterprises.* The wrought-iron words flew past, sending his mind awhirl. Why had they gone out of their way to drive past the building where his father had worked? Where he'd died? It was way off track from the way home.

Off to the side, glimpses of undulating sequins of light snared Heath's attention. Moonlight dancing on a broad expanse of water . . . silver luminescence topped with a hazy green mist.

Green Gas Lake? What was going on? Why had the men driven so far off course?

"Hey. Wr-Wrong way," Heath tried to tell the men in the front seat. What he hoped would be a loud protest came out a gurgled whisper.

Tepesh's private guards ignored his plea and kept talking to each other. The car turned again, leaving the asphalt road for a dirt trail with a rutted surface that forced them to slow a bit.

They jolted from rut to ridge to hole for a good distance before nearing an opening in the fence surrounding Dragon Enterprises. Smith maneuvered the big limo through and kept going, working his way to an open area far away from the rear of the big building.

As the car neared the edge of the lake, it began to slow. Heath's muffled attempts to get their attention finally worked.

"Looks like our passenger's getting a little antsy back there," the driver remarked with a snort of low laughter. "Bet he's thinking he should have quit after that little soda date."

Reilly turned slightly in the passenger seat, giving Heath a crooked smile. "Relax, kid. We're almost there."

The car slowed as it approached the edge of a five-foot drop where the lake kissed the end of Tepesh's business property. The driver punched his brakes and brought the vehicle to a stop. "Come on. Let's do this," he said, turning the motor off and opening his door.

Reilly popped his door and the two men moved to the rear door of the car where Heath was waiting, thoroughly confused.

Smith pulled Heath's door open. "Okay, kid, let's go. Just gonna take a little walk, get you some fresh air."

Heath wanted to tell them he didn't want any

fresh air; he just wanted to get home and go to bed, but the men were already pulling him out of the car and up on his feet before he could get the words from his mind to his mouth. He turned his attention to trying to make his feet work as the men hustled him around the open rear door and then toward the front of the car.

The ground was rough and unkempt, the uneven dirt and sparse grass bathed in puddles of moonlight and the glow of the car's headlights. Heath stumbled along, the hold the men had on his arms keeping him from falling as they kept walking forward.

"W-Weird," Heath muttered when the men stopped at the edge of the ridge, and he gazed out at the hazy green mist that hovered like a gossamer veil on the lake's broad expanse.

The words were barely out of his mouth when he felt a sharp pain to the back of his head and found himself hurtled into space. Surprise pulled a scream from his open mouth as he cartwheeled through nothingness. Seconds later, arms and legs flailing, he belly-flopped into the water, gulping in shock as the cold water closed around him.

CHAPER
†
ELEVEN

The water closed over Heath, rushing into his mouth and drowning out his startled cry. His mind was running wild, grasping for understanding. *Those bastards pushed me! What the hell!*

The shocking thought was gone in a micro-second as Heath gagged and swallowed convulsively, his body automatically fighting the foul-tasting liquid that slid down his throat. He suddenly realized he was going to drown if he didn't find his way to the surface fast.

Disoriented and not at all sure which way was up, Heath struggled to get himself upright in the ever-growing darkness of the water. As he sank lower still, he could feel his diaphragm convulsing more violently in a desperate attempt to pull in oxygen.

Flailing against the pressure of the water, Heath's panic escalated as his lungs fought harder to catch a breath. Panicked, he churned the water, turning his body in tight circular thrusts to search for a clue that would orient him. Bubbles rose around him and began to float gently upward. Heath's eyes followed their journey, grateful to see the green haze of the moon-lit mist over his head.

Up! Gotta go up! Heath thought, fighting the pull of the water with desperate strokes that began to propel him upward. He fleetingly wondered if the adrenalin coursing through his veins was responsible for somehow jolting his brain and body back to working order.

Fighting the water with desperate strokes, his body sliced through the chilled depths with more speed than he would have thought possible. He kept looking up, his heart pounding, his lungs screaming for oxygen as the light above him began to brighten.

Breaking the surface in a rush, Heath was propelled a foot into the verdant, mist-ridden night air before he fell back into water. The surface rippled outward with the force of his return to the lake's cold clutches. His struggle to suck oxygen into his protesting lungs was punctuated by racking coughs and convulsive gagging.

Finally, the coughing slowed and the muscles restricting his windpipe eased. Heath began to take in larger gulps of air that no longer led to vomiting up some of the swallowed water that had left a disgusting metallic taste in his mouth.

Heath treaded water until his breathing began to ease. When the gasps for air became something akin to normal breathing, he paddled himself around in a tight circle so he could look toward the ridge of land he'd been standing on mere minutes before.

He was shocked to find the crest of scrub-covered dirt empty of human life. And the limo's bright headlights no longer pierced the sky over the drop to the lake.

Stunned and confused, Heath stared at the now-empty spot he'd been launched from. "What the hell, man, what the hell!" he muttered. Skittering thoughts tumbled through his awakening brain. *What just happened? Have they gone for help? No, that makes no sense. They pushed me, dammit! They deliberately pushed me! They're not going after help. They're just gone.* He then felt the throbbing pain where he was struck on the back of his head.

"I gotta get out of here," Heath muttered, careful to keep his voice low even though he totally believed the two thugs who'd thrown him in the lake were gone. "But which direction should I take so I'll be closer to home?"

His brain seemed to be kicking into higher gear, a surprising shift of events considering how groggy and out of it he'd been just minutes before. Another turn in the water provided a panoramic view of his surroundings and gave him what he hoped was the correct answer in short order.

"That way," he said softly, staring at the far shore. "I think that's the correct direction. And now the question is, can I swim that far after all this?" Heath gave a resigned sigh. "Do I have a choice? Nope."

He immediately struck out for the chosen spot across the small lake, his strokes as strong as those of a professional marathon swimmer.

Far sooner than Heath expected, he was wading ashore. He stood on the shoreline for a moment, puzzling over how fast he'd been swimming and the surprising fact that he wasn't bone-tired and gasping for breath.

"Oh, well, amazing what wonders fear and a good dunking in cold water can work, I guess," he muttered. "And I need to be concentrating on what to do next."

Heath walked further up the shoreline and into a small bare area surrounded by trees. Once beneath their shelter, he bent and shook the water droplets from his hair then removed his wet shirt and wrung the water from it before putting the damp garment back on. He took one last look back at the lake and the building silhouetted against the night sky, the windows only small squares of light at that distance.

Doesn't look like anyone's around, he thought. *Maybe they just leave their office lights on at night, which probably means no one knows what happened out here.*

A new thought tugged at his mind. *Maybe that's a good thing. That was no prank. Those two guys deliberately threw me in the lake. And Tepesh – damn! What was it Tepesh said to them? Oh, yea. 'You know what to do.'*

"Son of a bitch," Heath muttered, stomping around the little clearing as his brain clicked away and memories of the evening began to return even more rapidly. "That bastard *ordered* those two flunkies to do what they did. I don't know why, but he obviously wanted me to drown! He wanted me dead! I'm going straight to the police when I get back to town."

Another rush of memories flooded Heath's mind – comments made by Tepesh and his son that shocked him badly now that he was thinking more clearly.

"No. No police," he cautioned himself, his pacing accelerating as he grew more agitated. "I can't contact them if there's any truth to what Tepesh said about higher-up officers on the police force being involved with his crazy plan."

Heath came to a quick stop and scrubbed a hand over his face as he suddenly remembered that Tepesh had sent flowers to their home after his dad's funeral. "And now he knows where Mom works. Son of a bitch!"

He wanted to scream his frustration. "He caused this. What if he might decide to hurt her if he finds out I'm still alive? I can't take that chance. So, what do I do now?" Frustration washed through him. "Who can I trust? No one, that's who."

His brain sparked again, and he suddenly had an answer for his dilemma. There *was* someone he could trust. Zoe. Dependable, ever faithful friend Zoe. All he had to do was get to her. Her parents' bedroom was downstairs in the back of the house. Zoe had the upstairs to herself. He remembered her commenting that her mom never went up there anymore; she just yelled up the stairs if she wanted to tell Zoe something. They'd never know he was there.

He just needed a little time to think things through, try to make some sense of the whole mess. If he went to Zoe's, he could lay low long enough to at least bounce some ideas off of her. She was always good at seeing things he didn't. Hopefully, the two of them would come up with a plan.

Feeling relieved that he at least had an immediate goal, Heath chose a direction he hoped would take him back to the city and started walking.

He pumped a fist in the air when he finally emerged from the woods bordering the lake and saw the dark sheen of the familiar asphalt-paved road ahead of him. It would take him through his neighborhood and on into Zoe's.

Feeling elated at his accomplishment, Heath increased his pace and before long he was surprised to realize he was running instead of walking.

Running faster than he'd ever run before.

§

Exhilaration flowed through Heath when Zoe's house came into view.

Within minutes he was standing beneath Zoe's window and wondering how he'd get her attention without waking her parents. Knocking on the door wasn't an option. How about throwing pebbles at her second-floor window?

Then the lattice-work trellis laced with honey-suckle near the corner of the house caught his eye and he sighed. *Perfect*, he thought. *I'll do it the tried-and-true teenage movie way.*

Scaling the tall structure was easier than he expected. At the top he hopped onto the section of the roof that covered the porch below, taking slow steps to avoid any creaks from the rafters supporting the over-hang as he carefully worked his way across the shingled surface.

Heath followed the slope of the roof until Zoe's bedroom window came into view, the full moon above reflected in the glass. He knelt in front of the window and carefully tapped on it. Seconds ticked by with no response. A worrisome thought blossomed in his mind. *Damn! What if she isn't home?* He tapped again, a little harder.

Moments later, from inside came the muted clatter of blinds being raised, and then Zoe's window slid upward.

"Heath, oh, my god! What are you doing out there?" she exclaimed in a hoarse whisper, her frightened face a pale oval as she reached out of the dark room to clasp his wrist. "Get in here before you fall!" She pushed the window higher still, and Heath gratefully climbed in.

Once Heath cleared the windowsill, Zoe poked her head out the window and scanned the street at the side of her family's house. "Where's your car?"

Heath shrugged. "I don't know."

Zoe opened her mouth to question his odd answer then changed her mind.

"Shut the window and make sure the blinds are closed. I'll turn on a light."

Heath turned to follow orders as Zoe headed across the room to her nightstand. He heard a click ,and the lamp immediately illuminated the room with a pale cone of light that left shadows in the corners.

Zoe turned and Heath noticed for the first time that she was wearing only an over-sized sleep shirt that hit her mid-thigh. He quickly averted his gaze and studiously scanned her room, noting the girly decorations and the hydrangea-dappled bedspread that she'd tossed to the end of her bed when his knocking woke her.

"Come sit down and tell me what's going on. I've been worried sick about you," Zoe scolded, walking over to pull out the desk chair and carry it back to the lighted area around her bed.

Heath obediently headed for the chair while Zoe plopped down on the bed and pulled a corner of the sheet over her legs.

Zoe's brow wrinkled as her eyebrows drew together. Frowning in confusion, she studied Heath from head to toe, taking in his wildly spiked hair, his terribly wrinkled clothes, and even momentarily staring at his face with a slightly puzzled look.

"Wow. That must have been some interview meeting," she finally said, remembering to keep her voice low. "What the heck went on? How'd your shirt get torn?"

Heath frowned. "Torn?" He ducked his head to check, running his hands up and down the front of his shirt. When he found nothing wrong except a vast expanse of wrinkles, he looked left and right, surprised to find gaping holes in the armhole seams of his shirt. He poked a finger in one of them, watching in confusion as the rip widened a bit more. "Dang," he said in surprise. "I didn't realize I was *this* much a mess. Guess the water did all this."

Zoe's frown deepened. "Water?" she repeated, obviously irritated that she wasn't able to make sense of Heath's rambling response. "What are you talking about?"

"Crap. Now I'll have to find a change of clothes," Heath said, clearly too focused on his wardrobe problems to pay attention to the question Zoe was asking.

Zoe threw her hands in the air and huffed in exasperation. "Oh, for heaven's sake, Heath. Sit still and be quiet. I'll be back in a minute," she instructed in a low voice as she stood.

Walking quickly to her bedroom door, she let herself out. The latch clicked softly as she carefully closed the door behind her.

Less than a dozen minutes passed before Zoe slipped in again, carrying an armload of men's clothes. Jeans, sweatpants, button shirts, and tee-shirts, even underwear and socks were dumped at the end of her rumpled bed. "There, that ought to do the trick," she told him, once again taking a seat on the side of her mattress.

"Damn, Zoe. Don't tell me you went downstairs and raided your father's closet."

She shook her head. "No. Of course not. These are my brother's clothes. Everything is still where it was when he died. Mom refuses to get rid of anything. Your good luck, I guess."

Heath felt a flash of worry. Hoping he hadn't accidentally re-opened Zoe's old wounds about her brother's death, he leaned forward enough to reach out and take her hand. "Thanks, Zoe."

Zoe clung to him for a few seconds then pulled away, all business again. "My brother was bigger than you, so they might be a little loose but anything would be better than what you've got on." She pointed to the half-open door across the room. "There's the bathroom. You can change in there. Grab what you want to wear, take a really quiet shower, and hurry back so you can tell me every single thing that happened to you tonight."

"I'll tell you," Heath muttered, standing and stooping to pick through the clothes Zoe had brought for him. "But you might not believe it."

Then he disappeared into the bathroom with a handful of garments, leaving Zoe sitting there with her mouth open.

CHAPTER
†
TWELVE

It took Heath only seconds to shuck his dirty clothes and step into the shower. Remembering Zoe's instructions, he turned the shower handle only enough to produce a gentle stream of water. Grabbing the bottle of bath gel from the hanging caddy on the shower head, he poured some into his hand and began vigorously scrubbing. It felt great to wash away the dust and sweat from his walk and the funky smell of the lake that lingered in his hair. The hint of a smile touched his lips when he realized the frothy bubbles smelled of vanilla, a scent he'd often noticed on Zoe. After rinsing, he stood under the water with his mouth open for another minute, swishing and spitting in an effort to wash away the lake water's lingering metallic taste.

As he moved his hand to turn off the water, he noticed the muscular definition in his forearm.

Heath turned off the water and exited the shower. With a quick glance in the mirror, he could see that his whole body had become more defined. When he stepped forward to pull a towel from a storage shelf loaded with fluffy towels and a variety of girly potions and lotions, his foot connected with something in the pocket of the dirty pants he'd left crumpled on the floor. Something small but substantial.

Damn! My cell phone! The water probably ruined it, Heath agonized as he grabbed the pants and stood butt naked and dripping wet to rummage through the pockets. Even as he extricated the phone from his pants, he couldn't help but hope that there was a chance, however slim, that something on the special recording disk David had put in his phone could be salvaged. He considered trying to turn it on for one brief moment but was too afraid that he'd accidentally do something that would render it totally useless if it wasn't already ruined by the dunking in that miserable little lake.

"David's really good with technical stuff. I'd better let him try to work some of his magic on this," Heath muttered softly to himself.

Phone in hand, he again reached for a towel, hurrying to wipe the outside of the phone dry. When he'd done all he could, he placed it on the vanity before pulling another towel from the shelf to dry himself. Then he quickly slipped on a pair of soft sweatpants and a tee-shirt. After hanging the damp towels over the shower rod to dry, he gathered up his discarded clothing, remembering to rescue his soggy billfold before he dumped everything in the wastebasket.

He took a moment to empty the wallet and spread its contents over the vanity to dry before grabbing the phone and exiting the bathroom to find Zoe waiting patiently on the side of her bed, right where he'd left her.

"Humm. They fit better than I thought they would. Good," she remarked as Heath crossed the room in his borrowed clothes.

"Look what I found," he said, holding the cell phone up for her to see. "But it went in the lake and I think it's probably ruined. I need to call David to see if he can do anything to save the recording."

Zoe made a face and shook her head for emphasis. "You can't call him at this time of night. It's way too late."

Heath wanted to argue against waiting, but he knew Zoe was right because of more than just the time. The things that had happened to him that night were weird, scary. He didn't understand the whats and whys of anything that had transpired.

Something in his brain warned him that he should be extra careful until he could get some sort of understanding of how things could have gone so wrong. Tepesh and his goons were still out there. Heath knew he'd be foolish to make another move until he untangled last night's bizarre events.

Zoe must have recognized the look of reluctant resignation on Heath's face. "Don't worry," she quickly assured. "We can call David in the morning after my folks leave. We'll have the house all to ourselves. Dad's got a business conference at some ultra-fancy hotel out of town, and Mom's decided to go with him. They plan to stay a couple of extra days and do a little sightseeing. They plan to be on the road by seven o'clock."

Heath nodded. "I know. You're right. We should get some sleep. I can tell you all about what happened in the morning." He glanced at the door to the hall. "Guess I can sneak into your brother's room."

Zoe's face clouded, and she quickly speared him with a determined look. "Are you kidding me? You said you'd tell me what happened tonight. I couldn't possibly go to sleep not knowing."

She scooted over on the bed, settled herself into a cross-legged position, and pulled her long tee-shirt over her knees. Then she patted the empty mattress beside her. "Come on. Get comfy and tell me everything."

Heath pondered the invitation for a moment and then thought, *What the hell, might as well get it over with. I'm not tired enough to sleep anyway no matter how late it is, and right now, I'm not crazy about the idea of being alone.*

"Okay, you win," he replied, pushing the pile of pillows on the empty side of the bed up against the headboard so he'd have something to lean against. Before joining Zoe, he made a silent vow to stay way over on his own side of the bed. Then he spent the next thirty-five minutes giving her a blow-by-blow description of the night's events.

"Well, I've got to admit it," she said when he finished the tale. You're right, that story's definitely hard to believe." She gave him a quizzical look. "Is this a joke of some kind? What's really going on?"

Heath sighed. "No, it's not a joke. I promise you, everything I told you is true. The question is what do I do now? If you have trouble believing me, how can I expect anyone else to?"

Zoe reached over and placed her hand on Heath's knee, her eyes full of concern. "I'm sorry. I shouldn't have popped off like that. Just give me a couple minutes to get all this straight in my head."

"Take your time," Heath replied with a touch of sarcasm.

Zoe sat silent, nibbling at her bottom lip as she apparently considered the validity of Heath's bizarre story. Finally, she asked, "Would you mind very much if we went over the high points again?"

"Sure," he managed to answer although he felt disappointed and more than a little irritated that she didn't immediately believe him. "Ask whatever you need to."

"Are you really sure that's what Tepesh said to the guys, about them knowing what to do? It's, huh . . ." She shot him an apologetic look. "It's not exactly 'take him out and kill him'."

"No, it's not. I don't know how to explain it – it was the tone of his voice, the look on his face," Heath replied, hoping his explanation was making some sense. "And the way the one guy answered. Sorta smug, like they were all privy to something I didn't know."

"Okay, next issue. Are you sure you only had the one drink?"

Heath nodded. "I'm sure. A jigger's worth at the most. Even if it was the strongest proof made, it shouldn't have knocked me on my can like that."

Zoe spread her hands out. "Well, seems to me like there'd only be one explanation for that. You were drugged. Remember, the butler did deliberately point out that specific bourbon bottle to you. It could have been spiked to begin with."

"Damn. I never thought about that. If that's what happened, it would explain a lot."

Zoe frowned. "Where was Victoria?"

"I never saw her," he confessed. "You don't think she had something to do with what happened, do you? Why would she do that when she's seemed really interested in helping, and it's pretty apparent she's pissed at her father. Why would she help him if that's the case? It doesn't make sense."

Zoe cocked her head to one side and speared Heath with a long look. "If you *really* understood what Tepesh and his son were talking about – all those comments about politics and vote-fixing and wealth-grabbing – then we need to at least consider the possibility. That's the family she was raised in, and I would think she'd be aware of what they're doing."

"I guess so," Heath said reluctantly, lifting both hands to rub his throbbing temples.

"I'm sorry, Heath. This has been a hell of a day for you. I know you believe what you're saying, and ... and well, I'm getting there. It's just that it's all so weird."

"Ha," he muttered. "You don't have tell *me* that. I know it sounds like something out of a bad sci-fi movie."

"You know what? We don't have to figure it out tonight. We can finish this discussion tomorrow. Maybe David can help make sense of it all." Zoe gave Heath's arm a reassuring pat before plumping up her pillow and scooting down in the bed. "I think it's time we both got some rest. Would you turn out the light, please?"

Heath doubted he'd do very much sleeping with his brain still trying to decipher the weird events of the night, but he reached over to do as Zoe asked. That's when he spotted the clock almost hidden behind the lamp on her nightstand.

"Is this clock right?" he asked, staring at the illuminated numerals showing a surprisingly earlier time than he expected.

"Yep." Zoe's answer was followed by a yawn. "Why?"

"N-Nothing. Just checking," he answered. The lamp clicked off and he lay awake for a long time, realizing he had more than water-logged phones to discuss with David come morning.

§

Dawn was breaking, the blinds throwing stripes of pale light against the wall on the far side of the bed when Heath awoke and was surprised to find Zoe, soft and warm and still sound asleep, spooned into the curve of his body.

So much for staying on my side of the bed, he

thought as he began the slow careful process of extricating himself. The last thing he wanted to do was have Zoe think less of him because she woke up to find her best guy friend snuggled up to her like some lech.

Heath had freed the arm she'd been resting her head on and managed to wiggle back to his side of the bed when Zoe sighed softly, stretched, and then turned toward him, all tousled hair and sleepy eyes. He felt his heart give an odd little bump.

Heat climbed Heath's cheeks. What was wrong with him? This was Zoe, his best girl buddy. Embarrassed, he quickly pushed the thought from his mind and wondered if he could manage to scoot any closer to his edge of the bed without falling off. He gave it a try and the bed creaked in response.

Zoe raised her arm, tapped a finger against lips curved with a soft smile then pointed downward in the direction of her parents' bedroom. Getting the message loud and clear, Heath nodded. They needed to be quiet until her parents left the house.

Obviously noticing Heath's discomfort, Zoe leaned in and whispered. "Don't worry. No one will check on me or expect me for breakfast. I always fix my own after they've gone."

"Got it," Heath whispered back, grateful there was no way she could know that what he'd been worrying about had nothing to do with her parents.

CHAPTER
†
THIRTEEN

"What's all this hush-hush stuff about? And why couldn't I tell anyone that I was coming to see Heath?" David asked the moment Zoe opened the door of her family's home.

"Heath's in the kitchen. It's better if he explains. Follow me," she replied, turning and leading David through the dining room and into the sunny kitchen where Heath, all bed-head hair and bare feet, was looking at a plate of scrambled eggs that he just could not eat.

Zoe scurried around the kitchen island to pour herself another glass of orange juice. "Want some?" she asked, holding her glass up to get David's attention.

David paused long enough to say, "Sure," then

he set his backpack on the countertop and plopped himself on the stool next to Heath. "Rad duds," he said, eyeing the form-fitting sweatpants and tee-shirt Heath had slept in. "They make you look all manly and beefed up.

"So, what's up? How'd the interview go?"

Heath swung around on his stool. "Thanks for coming so quickly. You brought your tools?"

"Yeah, I brought everything I thought I might need. Now, will you please tell me what's going on? And why couldn't I tell anyone that I was coming here to see you?"

Pushing his plate away, Heath took a deep breath. "Because Tepesh thinks I'm dead, and I think it's probably better that he keep thinking that for awhile."

David stared at his friend with a dumbfounded look. "Dead? What? I-I don't understand–" was all he managed to say before Heath cut him off.

"We're wasting time. There's my phone." Heath pointed to the device lying near a decorative bowl full of green apples on the corner of the granite counter. "Just see if you can fix it. Keep your fingers crossed that the recording feature worked. It'll explain everything."

David gave him a look that clearly conveyed he couldn't believe his friend had questioned his renowned techie skills. He leaned back, crossed his arms over his chest, and replied, "I'm betting that recording disk worked just fine. And I haven't come up against a phone I can't fix yet, you know that. So, what did you do to the phone? Drop it? Crack the screen?"

Heath shook his head. "Nope. I took a long swim in Green Gas Lake last night with the phone in my pants pocket."

Heath's answer, delivered so nonchalantly, made David's jaw drop. He reached up and nervously tugged the straggly patch of hair on his chin. "Damn. I can't fix that," he said, shaking his head. "That puppy's bound to be dead as a doornail. Forget the tools. I brought a spare phone with me. You didn't mess with anything inside your phone, did you?"

"No, I was afraid I'd do something that might erase the recording. I just dried the outside of the phone and left it alone," Heath assured.

"Good thinking," David muttered, opening up the outside case of Heath's phone and carefully extracting a little square card. "Zoe, can you hand me a clean dishtowel, please? A nice soft one."

Zoe complied and David went to work on the disk. "Looks dry now," he muttered after carefully dabbing at the little square shape for several minutes. He went back to work, spending a few more minutes dabbing and scrutinizing. Then he held the memory disk up to the light one more time, turning it every which way to make sure every centimeter of it was clean.

"So far, so good," David muttered to himself, laying the disk down and rummaging in his backpack for the extra phone he'd brought. He stripped it out of its protective bumper case, and after looking the disk over one more time, he opened the new phone and slipped the little square into place.

"Cross your fingers," he told Heath and Zoe, turning the phone on.

All three held their breath until the new cell blinked to life.

Heath let his breath out in a loud *swoosh* of air as Zoe exclaimed, "Yay!" and gifted David with a big smile.

"Yay for the phone working. Now let's see about the recording," David cautioned. He found the right icon on the phone's screen, tapped it, and they heard the sound of a car door closing.

"Oh, my god, it works!" Heath said, his voice full of relief. He gave David a congratulatory clap on the back. "I'll never doubt you again, my friend. I owe you one."

The recording played on, mostly silent for the first few minutes except for what Heath explained was the occasional brush of his footstep on the cement walkway leading to the porch. Then they heard the muted ring of a doorbell, and a few seconds later a man's voice said, "Good evening, sir. How may I help you?"

Heath's face lit up and he pumped his fist in the air. He looked at Zoe and gave a small nod of his head. "That's the butler. Just keep listening. Everything I told you is about to be confirmed."

An hour and a half later, Zoe and David heard Heath's surprised outcry, then the recording abruptly stopped. "And that's when they pushed me in the lake," he told his friends.

David tapped out of the program and pushed the phone aside. "Damn," he said softly. "Now I have a ton of questions. Like what happened after that, and how'd you get away from those two thugs? And how'd you get to Zoe's without your car?"

"By the time I resurfaced and got my bearings, they were gone, so I didn't have to get away from them. And I don't think they would have left if they didn't think I'd drowned in that lake. As for getting to Zoe's . . ." Heath lifted shoulders in a small shrug. ". . . I ran."

David looked shocked. "Ran? You mean you ran all that way? That's a lot of miles!"

Heath nodded. "I know. Close to twenty, I think."

"That's like running a marathon. It must have taken you hours."

"That's something else that's weird." Heath told them. "It didn't. When I noticed the time on Zoe's clock last night, I was shocked. I couldn't get the distance I'd run and the time that had passed to sync up at all. There's no way I should have been able to get here as fast as I did."

Zoe shot Heath a quizzical look. "But you didn't say a word about that last night. . . ."

"I didn't know how to explain it." Heath shrugged. "I still don't."

Zoe froze. "Oh, my god. Wait right here. I gotta go get something." Then she ran from the kitchen.

She was back in mere minutes, several sheets of paper clutched in her hand. "You gotta read these website pages I printed back when all this started up." She slapped the papers down in front of Heath and stabbed one section on the top page with a baby pink fingernail. "This couldn't possibly be true, could it?" she asked in a quivery voice as she watched him read the paragraph, her dark eyes full of worry.

As Heath finished each page, he passed it on to David, who mumbled swear words as he read. When he was finished, his gaze swung from Heath to Zoe and back again. "You've got to be kidding me.

Nazis? A mad scientist trying to make a super race? I'm with Zoe. How can this be?"

Heath expelled a deep sigh. "I don't know, but I'm beginning to worry that the Tepesh family experiments have come up with something."

"It could explain some of the changes," Zoe offered, her gaze searching Heath's face. "You're bigger." She frowned, spreading her hands as if to reach for an answer. "No, not bigger. Bulkier. More muscular. And your face looks a little different. More mature somehow."

David spun his stool toward Heath, peering at his friend for a long moment. "Damn. I think you're right, Zoe."

"We need to get you to a doctor," Zoe declared. "Now. Immediately."

Heath shook his head. "I don't think I can do that. It would be out on the news before we even left the office. We can't let Tepesh know we're on to what he's doing, and I sure don't want him to find out I'm still alive. The one thing we have in our favor is this recording. He doesn't know we've got it, and we can't do anything that'll let the cat out of the bag until we figure out how to use it."

The air seemed to go out of Zoe. She slumped against the counter, the very picture of surrender. "Okay, I guess you're right," she told him reluctantly.

"What we really need now is an emergency meeting with Stein, the sooner the better," Heath said. "This thing is bigger than we ever thought. He's got connections, and heaven only knows we need help."

"Heath's right," David said. "We need to call the professor."

"Okay, Heath. I suppose you're right," she told him reluctantly. "Make the call."

"I'll make the call as soon as these dishes are done. For everyone's safety, we have to be careful with every detail, including covering any evidence that I was here or anywhere else in town. Remember, I'm supposed to be dead."

CHAPTER

†

FOURTEEN

"Stein said he'd have Carter leave the side door unlocked," Heath explained as the three of them pulled into the restaurant's back parking lot. "They don't open for several hours, so we shouldn't run into any unexpected people."

Now clothed in jeans, a black shirt, and sneakers, Heath scanned the surrounding area one last time to make sure the lot was empty. The only vehicles he spotted were the professor's sedan and Carter King's catering truck. Just to be safe, he pulled the baseball cap Zoe had found in her brother's closet low on his forehead, casting a shadow on his face. "Okay. Let's go."

All three scrambled out of David's car and hurried to the restaurant door. Once inside, Heath, wary of his new and improved strength, carefully flipped the security lock to secure the door as Stein had instructed, and they headed for the back room.

Professor Stein was waiting for them, Carter King by his side. The five of them gathered around a table at the front of the room. Zoe gave Stein a copy of her printed website pages. The professor shook his head after reading them and passed the pages on to Carter, saying, "We can discuss this later. Let's see what the recording has to tell us."

David fired up the new cell phone and played the recording. They all sat stock still while listening, an occasional gasp or a word or two in an undecipherable mumble the only other sounds in the room.

When the playback was over, David tapped the phone off and Stein asked several questions similar to the ones David had asked back in Zoe's kitchen. Once again, Heath did his best to explain the unexplainable.

"Son of a bitch," Stein muttered when the room fell silent after Heath's last response. "This is worse than I expected. So much for having time to gather evidence before this fall's election. We need a plan of action now."

"Yeah, but what?" Heath asked. "We don't know enough about Tepesh's maneuverings to really be sure of what's going on. Everyone knows the Nazis worked on that super race stuff back in World War II. It didn't work then, maybe it still doesn't."

Stein shook his head and turned sympathetic eyes on Heath. "You're forgetting we've got more than a little evidence that it might be real. There was no proof back in World War II, but there's no way we can ignore what you experienced last night."

David nodded his agreement. "Don't forget, there've been rumors about stuff being dumped in that lake since Tepesh's company moved into the building," he reminded Heath. "You said you swallowed that water. Maybe that was enough to give you some super powers. . . ." David's statement faded away as he realized how unbelievable his words sounded.

Heath froze, his mind suddenly bombarded with scary thoughts. It really could be true. Hadn't he told Zoe and David exactly that just that morning? The look on his face went from fear to grim determination.

Sudden tears filled Zoe's eyes. She blinked them back and stayed very quiet.

The lull gave Stein a chance to take charge again. "Before we deal with that issue, there are a few things we need to take care of," Stein cautioned. He held up his hand and, finger by finger, began to tick off a list of essential needs. "One, get Heath's mom out of town for awhile, just to be safe. Two,

Carter's already got the Badger Brigade all set up. It's a group of individuals that, just like Carter, recognized that the country was about to be stolen by the super rich using the combination of right-wing media sources, bought and paid for politicians, and paramilitary units and decided to get trained in self-defense, weaponry, and tactics to prevent it."

"One transmission will do that, and I can send out a call to arms to locals whenever you say the word," Carter assured the group.

"Call to arms?" Heath repeated. "You don't really think–"

"I don't know what to think yet," Stein said. "But I do think we've got to be prepared for the worst."

"Wow," David muttered.

"Three," Stein said, clearly determined to continue with his points of action. "We need a way to verify or debunk the extent of this super race stuff and that probably means pulling Victoria into the planning."

Zoe's face turned stormy. "I don't think that'd be smart. We don't know if she can be trusted. She set up Heath's meeting with her father. And she's a person of privilege. It's more than a little possible that she could be part of the whole scheme."

Stein looked at Heath. "What's your impression?"

Heath shook his head. "I don't know. She's

always sounded so negative about her father, and she did offer to give us that list of names . . ." Heath's words trailed off.

The professor tapped a finger against his chin. "I've got an idea. She's supposed to bring the list in today. I can call her on some pretense – maybe move the meeting time up – and see if she really shows up with the names. Some face-to-face time might give us a better idea of where she truly stands. Then we'll know if we really need to shut her out of everything."

Heath exchanged questioning looks with Zoe and David.

"Can't hurt to try," David said with a shrug.

Zoe looked unhappy, but she grudgingly agreed that it might be a way to learn something while still maintaining Heath's safety.

"I'm going to step around the corner where it's quiet and make a call to Victoria," Stein said. "Heath, you be thinking of what sort of excuse you can come up with to convince your mom to leave town. But be sure not to tell her anything that happened to you last night."

§

"I figured it out," Heath said when the professor returned almost ten minutes later. "I called

Mom and told her I was going to be staying at David's 'cause we have a lot to work to do on a special research project for school. She hasn't taken a vacation since Dad died, and now she's got three weeks of vacation time coming that she'll lose if she doesn't take it soon. She's been talking about going to visit her sister, and I convinced her that this would be really good timing since I plan to be out of the house most of the time for the next week or two. Bottom line, she went for it."

"Perfect," said Stein.

"Yeah, she said she'd be packed and on her way within the hour. And she warned me that she was going to stay there at least two weeks, do some special stuff with her sister, and . . ." Heath had to grin at the small memory that popped into his mind. "She warned me to get to bed at a decent hour and pick a nice restaurant that serves plenty of vegetables if I decide to eat out instead of cooking for myself."

Heath's delivery of the line brought a small chuckle from the others.

"Good job," Stein told him. "That gives us some wiggle room on what to do next."

"Did you get Victoria?" Heath asked.

"I did," the professor told them. "And I got a very interesting response."

"What?" Heath asked, not at all sure he really wanted to know.

"Well, to begin with, she's plenty ticked off at you for not showing up for last night's appointment with her father."

Heath's jaw dropped. "Wh-What?"

"Yep. Unless she's the next Meryl Streep, she doesn't know you were ever there, and she's genuinely pissed at you. She certainly didn't mind letting me know that."

"But–"

Stein held up his hand. "There's more. She's going to meet me at my office in an hour . . . and she says she's bringing the list. What I need everyone to do now is lay low, stay on the QT, and plan to meet back here after closing time tonight. With a little luck, I'll be bringing Victoria's list back with me. Meanwhile, watch your back and stay alert."

CHAPTER
†
FIFTEEN

"Here's the list," Victoria said the minute she closed the door to Professor Stein's office. She handed several sheets of paper over his desk and quickly took a seat in the visitor's chair. It's the original list because my father will not allow me to have a cell phone or anything that can take a picture in the main house and the office copier makes too much noise.

"Thank you," Stein said, noticing the nervous way she clutched her hands in her lap as she waited for him to check what she'd brought. *Maybe she's afraid her father will discover she took it,* he thought, so eager to scan the names on the list that he gave only momentary thought to her odd behavior.

Leaning back in his chair long minutes later,

Stein again noticed how jumpy she was. "This will be immensely helpful, Victoria," he assured her. "I was aware of a lot of these people, but some of the names are quite a shock to me. At least we'll have a much better idea of who we're up against now. You were quite brave to provide this to us."

"I'm glad I could help. I know you'd probably like to ask some questions about the people on the list, but I have something I feel I should say, if that's okay." She quickly glanced at the professor then diverted her gaze again.

"Sure," Stein replied. "What's on your mind?"

"I want to apologize for getting in such a snit last night about Heath not showing up. I'm sure he has a good excuse, and I should have waited till I hear from him instead of taking it out on you."

Victoria's fluttery hands were moving from her lap to the chair arms and back again, and Stein was trying to analyze her unknowing confirmation that she still didn't know what had happened to Heath. Clearly, no one at the house had said a word about it to her. And that was very good for Heath's safety.

Stein searched for a way to put her worries at ease without giving away Heath's secret. "Thank you, Victoria. I appreciate what you've said," was the best he could come up with.

She looked up at him, the smile on her lips a bit tremulous, and again quickly shifted her gaze away.

"I, uh, there's something else . . ." She paused, drew a deep breath and, still looking anywhere but at Stein, continued. "Something else I *really* need to tell you." The words finally out, she momentarily glanced his way again, and he saw tears glistening in her eyes.

What's going on? Stein leaned back in his chair and twined his fingers together over his belt buckle, trying to put her at ease by looking relaxed and receptive to whatever she wanted to discuss.

"I don't know how to start, except to tell you that my father is a truly wicked man."

The look of anguish on Victoria's face made Stein afraid she might bolt from the room rather than continue, so he refrained from showing any reaction. "I'm listening," he said in a very calm voice. "You're safe here. You can tell me anything."

Victoria nodded. "For many years my father, and eventually my brother, worked on an experimental drug. They told Mother and me that the plan was to market it as a health supplement as soon as it was perfected. They always claimed it was going to be something that would make people better in every way. Much smarter *and* stronger physically." Victoria kept her eyes down while she spoke, only occasionally looking her professor's way as if to gauge how he was reacting to her story.

"Okay," Stein said, hoping his noncommittal response would keep the words flowing.

"But there was more to it than that, and I'm ashamed to say I think they designed it that way. Their initial plan was to market small doses of the supplement to very specific people – mostly Father's rich friends and people with the same attitude as he about the way the government should work. Anyway, with Gregor's help and a lot of experimenting, Father finally got the dosage just right, and all those people received a dose that did indeed provide the enhancement he'd promised them. But it was also quite addictive, so they had to keep paying a lot of money in order to maintain their new abilities, which suited Father just fine. The people apparently didn't care since they had untold buckets of money. And all along he and Gregor kept experimenting with the drug dosages."

"Sounds like he might have been after more than just money," Stein ventured.

"I heard my father talking to my brother one time, explaining to him that control was everything. With the supplement, they could control the world by controlling that small group of super rich people, who in turn controlled most of the world's resources." Victoria chanced another quick glance at her professor, obviously expecting a reaction of outrage. "When most of the rich, influential people they'd set out to attract were hooked on the supplement, Father discovered another means of control. He started wining and dining a number of big social media influencers."

Stein made sure to maintain a calm demeanor. "And . . ." he softly prompted.

"A lot of them fell right into line. Meanwhile, Father and Gregor discovered that different dose levels affected some of the people in strange new ways. Scary ways, sometimes," Victoria admitted with a choked sigh

"Too strong or maybe too smart?" Stein questioned.

"No," Victoria answered with a frown of remembrance. "More like so physically enhanced that smarter kind of went by the wayside. Those people got their physical strength bumped way up, but it also raised their inclination to violence. Basically, what they'd morphed into was a bunch of aggressive people wholly controlled by my father." She gave a bitter laugh. "Controlled, there's that word again. Anyway, what they become in the end depends on dosage and length of time they've been taking the drug."

"In what way?" Stein asked.

"Well, some developed ultra sensitivity to sunlight. They're stronger, brawnier, but they need protection from the rays of the sun. Then there's the biggest dose level, the level that was tried on people who wouldn't be missed like the rich and famous would be if things went wrong. . . ." With an agonized look on her face, she paused, clearly loath to reveal the rest.

Stein leaned forward, eager to learn more. "We need to know the whole story, Victoria."

"Something bad happened to the normal production of blood in a lot of the biggest dosage people. They eventually developed the need for fresh blood to keep them well. A lot of people were lost before they figured that out."

"Fresh blood?" Stein was totally shocked. "And what do you mean by *lost*?"

Victoria ducked her head. "I mean died. Many of the people they used to test those dosage levels died. Sometimes accidents were rigged to cover up a loss. Sometimes there were just too many for that. Sometimes they had no family so no one missed them. Sometimes families eventually went to the police and they wound up listed as missing. Bottom line, Father's got people who were willing to dispose of the bodies."

The professor scrubbed a hand across his chin. "Let me get this straight. Everyone who takes the supplement falls into those three categories?"

"Pretty much. Father calls the first group, which consists of his friends and business associates, 'the Elites.' Money is what they want. The second group is referred to as 'the Dragons.' Money's good, but they're really after control, domination of others. Then there's the group that Gregor laughingly started calling 'the Vampires' because of the need for blood. Misfits, mostly. People who belong to organizations like the White Supremists and the Neo Nazis, members of criminal gangs. People whose violent tendencies were elevated by the drug. Sometimes I wonder if my father deliberately planned those different levels."

Stunned, Stein was quiet for a moment. "How many of them are there?"

Victoria shrugged. "Hundreds, from what I can tell. All over the state."

Stein had to take a deep breath before he could continue. "How'd you find out about all this?"

Victoria shifted in her chair. "For a while I didn't know anything about the supplement except that they were going to produce and market it to the world in general if they ever perfected the dosage. Later, when I questioned them about disturbing conversations I'd heard between the two of them, they tried to pressure me into being involved in the whole horrible mess. I made it clear that I wanted no part of it, and for a while I thought Father'd given up on that idea. I'm sorry to admit, I didn't do much but hope that everything he and Gregor talked about wasn't really true." Victoria's eyes began to tear up again.

Fear speared through the professor. "Victoria, you didn't take any of that drug, did you?"

"No," she said, shaking her head. "I'd never do that. One time I even threatened to tell the authorities about what they were doing." Victoria began to tear up again. "That's when my father did a horrible thing. He started giving the supplement to my mother. Now she's addicted at the blood level. That's why he decided I needed to move here. He knows he has something to hold over my head now. He knows how much I love my mother. She had to have someone to help her, someone to make sure she gets blood when she needs it."

"And that someone is you."

Victoria wiped away a tear. "Yes. Father says she'll die if I don't."

Stein leaned forward, put his elbows on his desk, and massaged his forehead. "Well, we have a bigger problem than I ever imagined."

CHAPTER
†
SIXTEEN

Professor Stein was dealing with the monotony of grading papers when he decided to take a break from the boredom and check his phone for messages. His Signal app flashed a new message from an old friend. It was Simone Richards, a Systema Russian Martial Art instructor from whom he had taken self-defense lessons while living in DC Memories of long passionate dinners and discussions came to mind. Last he heard she was working on a law degree from Georgetown University.

"I need to see you," was all it said.

"When and where?" he said.

He kept looking at the app, hoping she would respond soon. He didn't have to wait long.

"Madison? Next Tuesday at eleven?" she asked.

"Done. Meet at Just Beans on State?" he said.

"Done," she said.

§

The ever-present scent of roast coffee invaded Stein's nose as he swung open the door to the coffeehouse. He shot a glance through the room but did not spot Simone. He walked over to the barista and asked for her whereabouts.

"Are you Jack Stein?" she asked.

"Yes," he said.

"Your visitor is downstairs," she said. "Follow me."

Stein navigated the small passageway between the counter and the wall till he got to the basement door. The barista opened the small door, and Stein squeezed into the stairwell. Squinting, due to the lack of light, he held the railings as he proceeded downward. Once reaching bottom he swerved right to avoid a crate of coffee. He then saw the slightly swinging lamp above a green-clothed poker table, and at the end the profile of a very attractive black woman sitting alone.

"Simone?"

"Jacob, oh my god, how long has it been?" she asked as they hugged.

"Too long," he said. "Still kicking ass in DC?"

"Well, yes, but not in DC and not in the way you think." They both sat down in the old saloon chairs.

"I finally finished my law degree and graduated with honors," she said.

Congratulations. So what's up? Why all the cloak and dagger?"

"I ran across a reference to you in my research. It was an article about the secret immortality research that Dr. Mengele was doing on prisoners and how that might have found its way into Tepesh pharmaceuticals."

"Wow, that's an old one," he said, sitting back in his chair. "I'm surprised you found it. Even the New York Times turned it into a blurb and buried it."

"We think it's real, and Tepesh is using it to recruit billionaires to help elect Walters," she said. "The promise of immortality is a strong aphrodisiac."

"Who's we?"

"Sorry. I guess I should back up for a bit. When I was in law school, I got an internship with the Southern Poverty Law Center. It was there that I began investigating rightwing fascist militia groups and found something extremely disturbing. I started noticing a pattern, certain names and links associated with funding these groups. Money is being funneled from Russia and other European and domestic oligarchs to groups like the NRA and individuals who then funnel it to these militias and certain politicians who work on behalf of the rich to restrict our voting rights. They are also buying up radio stations to broadcast their propaganda. These militia groups have been training for over thirty years. As you know, the Southern Poverty Law Center doesn't have a private intelligence or a security service. That's why when I graduated from law school, I formed NEMESIS, the National Emergency Missions Escalation Security Intelligence Service."

"Nemesis is also the name of the Greek Goddess of retributive justice," he said.

"You were always quite the wordsmith, Jack."

"According to SPLC, racists and far right followers have been going into the military and police for decades for training." She leaned forward, resting her arms on the table. "If you connect the dots, you get a history of individuals who have fallen through the cracks or if successful have been brainwashed in thinking the country is being taken over by baby-eating socialist pedophiles. I know it sounds stupid but the social media is all lit up about it."

"This is Hitler's playbook all over again." Jack shook his head in disbelief. "Back in the nineteen thirties there was a new social media called the radio and the Nazi's made sure every family had one. The problem was it only had one station and that was the Nazi station. While Hitler initially had only about a thirty percent or so following, his propaganda cemented the Nazi philosophy throughout the country and made one third of the nation hate another third of the nation, while the remaining third did nothing about it. This is also why in 1949 the FCC enacted the Fairness Doctrine, which basically stated that both sides of a political viewpoint needed to be presented in an equal amount of time so we wouldn't see a fascist takeover again. This was going well until Reagan came along and said he wouldn't enforce it. Then you had the rise of right wing talk radio, and that's when the propaganda began. Unfortunately, those on the left didn't bother to take notice. They thought no one would listen to it or believe it. Actually, initially rightwing talk didn't have much of an audience and was losing money, but then the rich benefactors came along because they knew they could use it to get politicians elected who would cut the taxes and gut regulations to increase their profits. It also eventually gave us the Citizens United decision, which further eroded our rights."

"Yes, this is part of a three-pronged process. First is media dominance, including radio and social media. Second, the purchase of like-minded politicians to further their fascist cause, along with packing the courts, and third is an alliance with far-right extremist militia groups," she said.

"Ok, but how is this going to figure in specifically in this election? Or any future election? This has been going on for sometime, probably since the adoption of the Southern Strategy. I think there has been some gains but not total control of the government. At most these groups go around intimidating people by showing up armed."

"That's not the point. It's not about an election. It's about an insurrection. It's about a full fascist takeover if they lose the election."

Jack placed his hands on the tabletop. "Now wait a minute, conspiracy theory much?"

Just hold on and listen. This is what I figured out so far. If they get the presidency, they would need to hold it for two terms to remove all the generals, agency heads, and pack the courts and all other relevant bodies. We came close to this before World War II with the Nazis in the US. Fortunately, back then there wasn't concealed carry and open carry. Also, the media was owned by numerous companies and individuals so there was no uniform voice, and we had many different opinions."

"They have been packing the courts for a while and even stole a supreme court seat from Obama. Rolling Stone wrote a great piece on that. So do you ever wonder why those Nazi bunds faded away?"

"My guess was when we entered the war," she said.

"Well, in some places they faded before then. There were about twenty thousand of them in New York. It became a big concern for the Jewish community, who worried that what happened in Germany could happen here. One Jewish leader was a former congressman. He contacted mob boss Meyer Lansky about Jews demonstrating more militancy. Lansky was told that money and legal services would be put at his disposal if he could make sure the Nazis were beaten up but not killed. Lansky refused the money and assistance and said he would handle the situation. His crew went around breaking legs and cracking skulls. This reduced the Nazi's attendance at their meetings and the wearing of their Nazi uniforms. Pretty much making them ineffective. Contrast that to what happened in Italy and Germany. In Italy the fascists would beat anyone they didn't like, such as the socialists. People felt intimidated by them. In Germany Hitler, with his strong anti-Semitic convictions, argued that Germany had been defeated in World War I because of weak leadership, Jewish and Communist influences in the government, along with an international conspiracy. His paramilitary group was the Brown Shirts. In 1923 he announced he wanted to overthrow the government, but his insurrection failed. He and his followers were given light jail sentences, which allowed him to eventually seize power again. Violence works."

"True. What I learned from my years studying violence prevention is that the perception of violence is stronger than the act of violence. When people hear what happened, a large number of people will not do anything that may lead them to go to the hospital. The question to ask is why isn't this happening now? Why isn't any group trying to stop these fascists this way? The answer is that they learned they could get their butt kicked if the people stood up to them. That's why over the years they've been loosening gun laws in every state."

Jack nodded. "I didn't think about that but now it makes sense. People will see some idiot prancing around with an AR-15 and try to avoid him. Plus, now they made fully armed militia training possible and enticing, with the brainwashing from right wing talk radio. It's the only way the rich can stay in power. More and more countries are turning to fascism as the rich are starting to consolidate their power to stay in charge. Of course, throw in a healthy dose of lies, hatred, and racism and you have an army. My guess is Tepesh has been doing this for a while. If he gets the presidency through making Walters president, he can rule the world. However, if we expose his immortality plot, no way will Walters win."

"No, Jack, he's created a following of ultra-religious nationalists who believe the country is so bad off they are willing to die for their leader. All he has to do is say that the election has been stolen and they will try an insurrection."

"Try, perhaps, but there is no way he would win except if there are enough people on the inside of the government that would help him. So what is the answer?

"Tepesh must be arrested and exposed," she said.

Jack crossed his arms. "That is easier said than done."

"That's where NEMISES. comes in. I've been working with Carter, and through both of our contacts, we developed our own security force. He calls it the Badger Brigade. We have investigators following Dragemore around, but you've got his daughter and that is the best inside card to play."

"Let me know what I can do," he said.

"Will do."

Both got up from their chairs and with one parting glance, hugged each other before heading up the stairs.

§

In a few days the group met. "Let's get started...."

Stein and Carter were already there when Heath, Zoe, and David slipped into Just Beans that night. Sitting quietly off to the side was a woman none of the three recognized. Heath guessed that the woman, medium height, blonde, brown-eyed, and attractive, was in her late thirties or early forties. He had no idea what she was there for.

Catching the exchange of questioning glances between the three friends, Stein took his place in front of the big table and began the meeting almost immediately. "Let's get started. Good news is, Victoria brought the list, and it's going to be very valuable in our fight against the evil ambitions plaguing our nation. The bad news is this. . . ." And he proceeded to tell them everything that Victoria had told him that afternoon.

When the professor finished, Heath sat very still, anger and despair coursing through him as he thought of his father's death and how the company had blocked every attempt he and his mother made to gain information about the accident. Now he knew why.

Apparently caught up in his own thoughts and fears after hearing what Victoria had told the professor, David's hand shook like that of a palsied old man as he raised his coffee cup to take a drink, while Zoe, always more attuned to Heath's feelings, simply muttered a soft "Oh, my god" before reaching out to clasp his hand.

Stein nodded then turned to acknowledge the newcomer, who'd sat quietly through his revelations about Tepesh and his cult of money-hungry traitors. "That's why I asked Carter to invite Simone Richards to join us tonight," the professor explained. "She's the head of NEMISES, a non-profit she founded to investigate and stop threats to our democracy. She's got the contacts and the knowledge to help us. The question now is, considering this almost supernatural army Tepesh's supplement has produced, how do we attack the problem?"

"What if we took the story to the press? The whole story, life-changing supplement, vampires and all," Heath questioned.

"It might help some, but you have to consider the fact that a lot of those big newspapers are owned by the very multi-billionaires Tepesh has already turned," Stein reminded them. "They'd squash that story like a bug."

"How about the Freedom Press Syndicate?" Heath ventured. "And Channel 19. They're both independent, and as far as I know, neither of them have ever backed off of a story vital to the nation's well-being."

"Good thinking," the professor said. "We need to keep them in mind for when we want to break the story. Simone, why don't you join me up here so you can share any other ideas you've got about the situation."

The woman nodded, then stood and walked to the area where Stein had been pacing as he talked. She smoothed the back of her stylish navy skirt before quietly taking a comfy leaning position against the big table.

"You've got the floor," Stein told her, moving off to the side a bit.

"As I'm sure you well know, we've definitely got a big problem to deal with," she began. "Not only how to stop Tepesh and his followers, but how to do it without scaring the hell out of our citizens. Vampires, zombies, whatever, all that supernatural stuff makes great entertainment for television, but no one wants to believe it could possibly be real."

"We gotta do something," Zoe declared. "With the rich people and the politicians Tepesh already owns, if he gets this win, he'll control our country. And if he controls this country, he controls most of the world, and he'll suck all the profit out of it. There will only be serfs and masters. A new plutocracy."

"More like a slave-ocracy," David muttered.

The professor stepped back to the center. "Sorry, guys. I forgot to tell you about the last part of my conversation with Victoria. She had one more piece of news to share before she left my office. She told me that her father's hosting a huge fundraiser at their home a week from now. Most of the people on the list will be there, so he's pulling out all stops.

He expects millions in contributions to be made to Walters' campaign."

Simone looked more than a little concerned. "That big a cash infusion is really bad. We've got to move faster than I expected."

"There's more," Stein cautioned. "Tepesh has big plans for a social media campaign. He plans to have the attendees with the most social media appeal endorse Walters and encourage their followers to vote for him. He's going to have all those endorsements video-taped so he can blanket the airways and the Internet with ads. And we all know what bombardment by social media can do."

"No matter the cost, he's got to be stopped," Heath told them, the words delivered through gritted teeth.

Carter left his usual post by the door to join Simone. "Guys, I'm aware that time is really tight, but I happen to know that in the past Simone has pulled off some mighty big capers on a very tight schedule." He turned to her and asked, "What do you think the chances are for doing that this time?"

"Challenging, but possible. At least there's something to work with. A big, heavily attended party requires a huge number of service people. The caterer's servers, limo drivers, valets, musicians – we've got well trained people who can fill those slots, people experienced in undercover tactics, such as casing a place, eavesdropping on attendee conversations, and picking up more clues than you'd ever imagine in a party like that," Simone told them. "Keep in mind that this would be strictly for gathering information, not some sneak attack. We need all the info we can get before we plan anything like that."

"Wow," David said, obviously thoroughly impressed.

"You really think you can pull something like that off with such short notice?" Heath questioned.

Simone smiled. "I assure you, my people can perform all sorts of miracles. However, to make this one work, we've got one more piece of information to obtain, and that'll require Victoria's help."

"What's that?" Stein asked, his brow furrowed in concentration.

"Information on the layout of the house, diagrams if possible, an idea of what events will take place in which rooms, number of security people, etc. Information that's vital in order to prepare our undercover people to the best of our ability. We sure as hell don't want to do anything that would alert Tepesh that we're on to him."

"You're absolutely right," Stein agreed.

"If we do this, Victoria will have to come to the next planning meeting, and we'll have to tell her what we're working on," Simone warned. "She'll need to be available at least that once to answer any additional questions we need to address."

Simone turned slightly and her brown eyes searched Heath's face for a long moment before she continued speaking. "It'll also mean letting her in on the secret that you're alive. Do you have any objections to that, Heath? Do you think you'll feel safe if she knows? And do you believe we can we trust her to not betray us?'"

Everybody's eyes turned to Heath.

Heath didn't even hesitate before answering. "After what she's already revealed, I believe the answer is yes. And I can live with anything as long as there's a chance of making that son-of-a-bitch pay for what he did to my dad."

CHAPTER
†
SEVENTEEN

For a whirlwind week, the six-member core group of the BPO, the Blue Paperclip Organization, spent every spare moment either studying the diagrams and notes Victoria had gladly provided, being tutored by Simone's people for the roles they each would play, or learning self-defense moves taught by a pro connected to Simone's agency. Heath discovered that his new strength required him to hold back when practicing defensive moves. Whatever his episode in the lake had done to him, the enhanced strength and extra stamina were still there.

For varied amounts of time, whether day or night, the skilled professionals of Simonoe's agency's met with the BPO people in a rented safehouse procured by Simone, coaching them in proper job tasks and service attitudes for the roles they'd been assigned and fitting them with Hollywood-quality disguises designed to protect their identities and prevent party goers from suspecting they were anything other than what they pretended to be.

Each of them knew what roles the other members of their team would be playing. And, just to be safe, a few key people in Simone's group would wear blue paperclips in inconspicuous places. They all hoped there'd be no reason for anyone to need help the night of the party.

Stein and Simone would pose as event managers for the catering team, Carter would be the man in charge of valet parking, Zoe was assigned to the catering staff, and David tutored Heath for his role as hired event photographer as well as working with the agency's sound team, who would wire the attendees and listen on the night of the party from some nearby safe location to everything their mics picked up. All participants would be on alert as they worked the party, although Zoe and Heath would have the most freedom to move about the various rooms.

Because of her mother's problems, Victoria had already served as her father's hostess for a number of months. The importance of maintaining a normal atmosphere at the house exempted her from participation at the safehouse. All Simone expected of her was to be alert and aware until the party was over.

For the four additional nights Zoe's parents were gone, Heath stayed with Zoe so they could continue developing their assigned character roles. Exhausted, they would crawl into Zoe's big bed and reminisce about the "good ol' days" when life was normal and innocent. Heath grew used to finding Zoe cuddled in his arms come morning. He knew he would miss her when her parents returned and reluctantly admitted to himself that would be wiser to stay with David or sneak into his own house for a few hours of restless sleep than mess up the whole plan by taking a chance of being discovered by the McGoverns when they returned.

§

On the big night, dressed in a fancy tux, a brown wig streaked with gray, horn-rimmed glasses with no correction in the lenses, and padding over the six-pack abs he'd developed since his dunking, Heath was the perfect picture of a middle-aged man. There were flutters in his stomach as he eased the rental Lincoln sedan the professor had arranged for him up to the gated entrance of the Tepesh mansion, in the time slot allotted for all the hired help to arrive. As he once again waited for a guard to come out of the fancy little shack, he fervently hoped it wouldn't be the same guy who'd checked him in before.

A different man emerged, and Heath drew a relieved breath. "John Morris, photographer," he told the guard in the slightly southern twang he'd practiced long and hard with the voice coach.

The guard checked the clipboard in his hand and waved him on. Heath breathed a little easier as he drove through the gate.

Maintaining a slow speed as he once again followed the winding road to the house, he noticed an increased number of the black-uniformed guards he'd seen patrolling the grounds the first time he made the trip. "Lots more security people, as expected," Heath said aloud, glad to know David was with the sound crew somewhere in the vicinity, listening to every word he uttered. "Almost to the valet stand. I can see Carter now."

Heath pulled up to the designated spot and powered down the driver's side window.

"Good evening, sir," Carter greeted, bending and casually resting an arm on the bottom of the car's window frame. The name stitched above the pocket on his blue uniform shirt read Roger Evans. "Pull around back to the rear entrance parking lot. Valets will be there to direct you where to park your car. Ask for Marsha Threadstone or Leonard Brown once you're inside. They're the event managers who will give you your final instructions," Carter informed Heath in a perfectly business-like manner. Then he straightened and nonchalantly waved him on.

At the rear of the house, the drive ended in a large parking area already filled with equipment rental company trucks and half-a-dozen catering vans, some with their back doors open and ramps still in position. There were also a number of vehicles that Heath guessed probably belonged to other various service people working the party.

Two valet attendants were watching dozens and dozens of delicate gilded chairs being unloaded from one of the rental company trucks. Once out, they were stacked on dollies and pushed to the house's back entrance.

Heath stopped and lowered his window again. "Any particular area?" he asked.

"No, sir," the taller man answered. "Just don't block any of the rental equipment or catering trucks. They're still unloading all sorts of stuff."

"Understood," Heath said.

"When you get to the door, just go on in. You know who to ask for?"

"I do. Thanks." Heath replied, raising the window and driving to an area just past all the trucks emblazoned with the caterer's logo.

Once parked, he grabbed the expensive digital

camera David had taught him how to use and exited the car. The clang of metal and a rattle of wheels alerted Heath that another big service cart had been offloaded from one of the catering vans and was on its way to the kitchen. He quickly hurried ahead to hold the door open so the two men pushing the heavy load could maneuver past him and into what turned out to be the biggest, fanciest kitchen he had ever seen.

The room was filled with catering staff, all scurrying to set out prepared plates of hors d'oeuvres and pastries, while a rotund chef outfitted in white coat and high hat gave the big pots on the eight-burner stove an occasional stir and periodically checked the contents of the built-in ovens. On the far side of the room, two women were busy removing the last of rental linens from a rolling container. The room was filled with a virtual cornucopia of aromas.

"Uh, I'm looking for Marsha Threadstone. Can you point me in her direction?" Heath asked a waiter as he scurried past with a trolley loaded with crates of rental wine glasses.

"Dining room," the man replied, tilting his head to indicate which direction.

Heath told him thanks and headed for the nearest door. It turned out to be the entrance to a huge butler's pantry. Glass-fronted cabinets held several sets of expensive china and multiple types of goblets and glasses. *Worth a small fortune*, he thought with a shake of his head.

He was musing over the two doors on the far wall when one of the women pushed the empty linen cart into the room. She flashed a quick smile and hurried off, leaving Heath alone again. He tried the first door and found it opened into a storage closet full of vacuums, mops, and various cleaning supplies. The second door led to a hall where one turn and a short walk down another hall took him to the dining room entrance.

He found Simone in the palatial room, issuing instructions to wait staff setting up a buffet fit for royalty on an unbelievably huge dining table. He saw almost no resemblance to the woman he'd met a week ago.

The air in the room was perfumed by the gorgeous centerpieces of peonies, lilies, and delicate pink roses in silver bowls positioned down the long length of the elegant table.

"Miss Threadstone?" Heath asked as he held up his camera. "I'm John Morris."

Simone turned, the skirt of her fancy chiffon cocktail dress rippling with her movement. She checked the tiny gold watch on her wrist. "Excellent. We've got almost half an hour before the party starts. I was told you've been doing events of this type for a long time, so why don't you just wander around, check the rooms and identify places that would make the best backdrops for the guest photos."

"Sounds like a plan," he replied with a nod.

"No, no. Not this room," Simone said, turning away from Heath to intercept one of the florist's staff carrying an arrangement of purple orchids. "All of those arrangements go in the formal living room." She pointed to a large arched entrance. "That way."

The florist hurried off, and Simone went back to issuing orders regarding the assortment of large trays and bowls being placed on the table.

Taking his cue, Heath ambled out of the dining room, receiving a quick nod of recognition from Stein in his event-manager tux and very authentic-looking beard and wig as they passed each other in the hall. Heath stayed in character, continuing his theoretical search for perfect photo spots without the slightest bobble. He planned to check every room he could – except the study. No way did he want to go in that room again.

Drawing on memories of the diagrams Victoria had furnished, Heath began exploring the other rooms on the ground floor, noting exits to the outside in case of an unexpected emergency, and counting the number of house staff he encountered along the way. He discovered a string quartet tuning up near the main hallway entrance to the mammoth orchid-filled living room.

Back in the main hallway, he paused to eye the grand staircase leading to the second floor. Although he knew he could get away with using the stairs as a way to position bigger groups of guests, he could think of no plausible reason for going upstairs to check for additional photo spots.

He assumed Victoria was still up there, getting ready for the guests to arrive. He hadn't seen her since the day she'd come to the first real planning meeting Simone headed, to provide the diagrams and information Carter's agent friend had requested. Victoria had been devastated by the tale of Heath's ordeal and had apologized over and over again, swearing she knew nothing of what her father had planned. Her anguish was so obvious, no one, least of all Heath, had a problem believing her.

At the end of that meeting, Simone had instructed Victoria to stay home, act as normal as possible, and keep her eyes and ears open for any scrap of information she could garner, particularly the smallest hint that her father had somehow caught wind of their plans. Heath had agreed. After all, he had first-hand knowledge that her father was capable of anything. He knew Victoria was going to have to walk on eggshells until the danger from Dragomere Tepesh was neutralized.

Heath was hanging out in the breakfast nook – bigger than his mom's kitchen and dining room put together – when he heard the doorbell ring and caught a glimpse of the butler scurrying down the hall to greet the first guests. Much as he hated the thought of being around the guy who, according to the recording, had simply held the door and watched Dragomere's goons drag him off to be "disposed of," he figured that any experienced photographer would snap photos of the rich and renowned as they entered. And, to be safe, Heath surmised, he had no choice but to act like a genuine photographer and go take those arrival photos. He salved his discomfort with the thought that he'd be able to snap pictures of every single guest who attended the party. Simone would appreciate the effort since it would make tracking Tepesh's people easier when the time came.

Heart beating a little faster, Heath took courage in hand and followed the butler to the front door. Before the man opened the door for the first arrivals, he turned and gave Heath an up-and-down look that sent his nerves skittering.

The bell rang again and the butler abandoned his perusal to welcome the first batch of guests. Heath quickly busied himself with posing the people for group shots or couple shots, all the while aware of the butler's periodic scrutiny. Apparently satisfied that the hired help was doing a proper job, the man eventually turned his back on Heath and concentrated on the doorbell that rang almost continually.

Heath gave himself a mental pat on the back for choosing to shoot the arrival photos despite the proximity of the butler when he overheard the man tell a guest that Mr. Tepesh was in the library where they were video-taping the endorsement ads. Heath hoped Victoria's father would stay in there all evening. He had no desire to spend even the barest amount of time with him again.

As soon as the arrivals dwindled to nothing, Heath returned to the living room, roaming through the crowd, smiling big and snapping photos of various dressed-to-the-teeth people. He handled it like a seasoned pro, complimenting the ladies' designer dresses and elaborate jewelry, prompting people to turn, smile, tilt their head a bit, or asking them to say something silly like "Say caviar" to make them laugh for the picture.

Rich socialites, business moguls, and busy wait-staff with trays of dainty hors d'oeuvres or delicate crystal wine stems and hefty tumblers filled with whatever special alcoholic concoction some guest had ordered ebbed and flowed through the room, a sea of ebony tuxes, colorful gowns, and service people in black pants and starched white shirts.

Near the scheduled end of the evening, Heath took a breather long enough to tuck himself into one of the rented gilt chairs in a quiet corner and down a Perrier with a splash of lime – the only non-alcoholic beverage provided. He was relieved to finally catch a glimpse of Zoe as she slipped through the room, tray in hand, bright-eyed and perky in her black and white service uniform.

Once Zoe disappeared from view, Heath returned to casually scanning the room, beginning to wonder if Victoria had even come downstairs yet. There was always a chance she was in the library with her father, but Heath had thought she'd probably try to mingle with the crowd enough to assure some of the BPO people that things were still under control.

A flash of emerald green caught his eye as a woman walked past the entrance to the hallway. Victoria? Maybe. There was something about the way the woman had carried herself that made him think it might be. Heath quickly deposited his empty glass on the tray of a passing waiter and hurried off in pursuit of the young lady.

He caught up with her just as she neared the staircase. "Miss Tepesh?" he called before she could climb the first step and was relieved when the woman stopped and turned so he could see that it really was Victoria. "I thought you might like a memento of this special evening?" He held the camera out, expecting her to play the part of happy hostess, to smile and agree with enthusiasm.

But Victoria didn't respond as expected, and it threw Heath for a loop. Something was wrong. She held herself still and stiff. And there was an odd look in her eyes. Not fear, more like sadness or quiet desperation.

At a loss for words, Heath was still trying to decipher what might be bothering her when Victoria seemed to physically pull herself together and step back into expected behavior.

"I'd love a picture!" she gushed, lifting the skirt of her gown a bit and swishing the gossamer fabric in a fluttery arc. "Daddy bought me this beautiful dress and it would be simply perfect to have a photo of me in it to frame for his desk."

Alarm bells went off like crazy in Heath's mind. *Daddy?* He'd never heard Victoria refer to Tepesh as anything but Father. And the ultra-animated way she'd responded, like some silly, empty-headed debutante – that was nothing like her normal way of speaking.

"I've got the perfect place for the picture. Follow me," Victoria said, turning in an emerald swirl and hurrying off without a backward glance.

Heath gave a mental shrug and went in pursuit. Off to the side near the back of the house, Victoria led Heath into a beautiful glass-enclosed sunroom filled with exquisite white wicker furniture. Beautiful potted plants were scattered around the edge of the room.

Victoria made a full turn. "Marvelous, we've got it all to ourselves," she exclaimed. "I can sit on the glider; it has all those lovely blooming plants behind it. Perfect background, wouldn't you agree?" She hurried off to the charming little glider and took a seat. "Come closer," she called. "I want the beading on my dress's bodice to really show up."

"Of course, Miss Tepesh," he agreed, still puzzled by just about everything. He went down on one knee, and began testing angles and lighting for the would-be photo.

Victoria lowered her head and watched her hands as she casually spread out the full skirt of her gown. "Keep the act up," she whispered, giving the skirt a tug here and a pat there in a pretend effort to better show off its beauty. "Don't do anything that would make this look suspicious. If there's anyone in the garden, they can see us, but they can't hear us."

Oh, hell, something's really wrong, Heath thought.

"Don't worry, Father doesn't suspect anything about this evening. I'm the one in trouble."

Heath snapped a photo. "Looks good. Let's try

it from a slightly different angle," he said at normal volume. He stood and changed position, stopping to fiddle with the camera again while he waited for whatever else Victoria was trying to tell him.

"It's my mother and me."

Click went the camera.

"My father told me that he's sending me to Europe to marry that man he picked out for me. He's got Gregor working on a private flight to take me, probably by the end of the week. And he plans to put my mother in an asylum since I won't be here to care for her." She sniffed a little, forced a smile, and changed poses for the camera.

Click. Click.

Heath was stunned by what she'd said. It was all he could do to stay quiet and hear her out.

"He says he's got too many important things to handle right now to bother with either of us."

She lifted her head again and Heath caught the sheen of tears in her eyes.

Click.

"There's gotta be something we can do," he said, moving slightly to shoot from another angle.

"I don't think so," she whispered, turning and pretending to preen for more shots. "There's no way I can get past the guards. He's given them orders that I not be allowed to leave the house."

Click.

There's no way I can let that happen, Heath thought, desperately scrambling for a solution.

Suddenly, he remembered the roller container half-full of rented linens – tablecloths, napkins, and towels and cloths for clean-up – and he had a crazy idea. Crazy enough that it just might work.

Click, click went the camera, giving him a chance to look at his watch before he lowered his arm again. If the crew wasn't already beginning to pack up, they would be soon.

Heath began to fiddle with the camera again. "Listen to me and don't argue. Just do as I say. Understand?" he whispered.

Victoria looked confused, but she quickly changed poses and nodded.

"Meet me in the butler's pantry in ten minutes," he told her, remembering to keep his voice low and controlled. "Try not to talk to anyone on the way. There's a storage closet there. Get in it and don't move a muscle until I come for you. Can you do that?"

"Yes," the word came out all trembly, but at least her tears were gone and there was a hint of hope in her eyes.

"These should turn out great," Heath told Victoria, back to normal volume. "I'll have proofs for you in a few days and you can pick the ones you want."

She managed a smile that looked more like

her old self. "Thank you so much. I look forward to meeting with you again. Good night," she said, and Heath knew she was letting him know she'd do as he instructed. Before he could say anything else, she lifted the skirt of her gown and hurried out of the room.

Heath took a deep breath and immediately headed for the kitchen in search of Professor Stein. When he found him busy returning stemware to a sectioned crate, he paused behind him, pretending he was absorbed with brushing something from his lapel. "Which van are you driving?" he asked Stein in a whisper.

The professor kept working on the glasses. "First one on the right. Why?"

"Later," Heath replied. "Try to tell everyone to get packed and out as fast as possible."

Message delivered, it took Heath only seconds to disappear into the pantry, which he thankfully found empty. The cart was still where the woman had left it, only now it was half-filled with a haphazard array of rumpled linens. He threw one last look over his shoulder then crossed the room. Relief swept through him when he cracked the storage closet door and spotted Victoria huddling in the far corner of the dark closet.

"Come on," he quietly urged. "Hurry." He turned and grabbed all the linens he could reach, tossing them in a high heap to the far side of the container. "Get in, crouch down and don't move a muscle until you're told it's clear."

Victoria never questioned the odd order; she simply scampered out and climbed in as fast as she could. She was barely in place when Heath began grabbing handfuls from the linen heap to pile on top of her.

Tucking his camera into a corner, he pushed the cart into the kitchen. "I'm going out for a break," he told Stein, thinking that had to be a standard and unquestionable reason for someone to want to go outside all of a sudden. "Thought I could go ahead and get this out of your way, if you want."

The professor feigned surprise. "Why, thank you. It's always nice to have extra help." He stepped over to open the back door.

Heath gave him a nod and put his enhanced strength to good use, pushing the cart right out the door and straight to the catering van.

CHAPTER
†
EIGHTEEN

"I get it. It was foolish and dangerous, but I probably would have done the same thing," Simone told Heath. "But now we have to face the fact that this changes everything."

Clearly troubled by a situation filled with the unknown, Simone slowly paced around the rental house's well-used dining table which was occupied by the five who'd attended Tepesh's grand party, plus David, and the woman whose problem had become theirs. Role-playing attire had been abandoned in favor of more comfortable clothing, and Victoria had exchanged her fancy gown for a pair of yoga pants and a man's tee-shirt so big that one side of the neck opening hung on the point of her shoulder. The agency professionals who'd helped them prepare for the party were gone, and the house was quiet except for the monotonous sound of Simone's footsteps.

Heath ducked his head, thinking he probably should say he was sorry, but the knowledge that he really didn't regret what he'd done made the words stick in his throat. No one with a drop of compassion could have left Victoria in that situation.

Breathing a soft sigh of resignation, Simone pivoted and returned to the empty seat at the head of the table. She sat down and placed the tablet and pen she'd been carrying on the tabletop and turned her attention to Victoria. "Well, what's done is done. Now we need to figure out what the consequences might be and how to prepare for them."

Below the table, Zoe reached over and gave Heath's knee a sympathetic pat. Relieved that at least she understood, he gratefully twined his fingers with hers.

"We'll tackle this one issue at a time. You ready for some questions, Victoria?" Simone asked.

Victoria gnawed at her lip and nodded yes.

"This situation with your mother; how's that going to be handled?"

"Knowing my father, he'll probably have Charles take care of everything."

"Who's Charles?" Simone questioned.

"Sorry. He's the butler," Victoria responded, the

haggard look on her face revealing how distraught she was about her mother's future fate.

"Did he tell you when she'd be moved?" Simone asked, scribbling notes from Victoria's previous answers.

"Not exactly. He just said it would be in the next couple of days. The plan was to have her gone before I left for . . ." Victoria took a deep breath and forced the words out. ". . . left for Europe."

"But she's at the mansion now, correct?"

Victoria nodded.

"Her being there, does that require any special help?" Simone asked. "A nurse or companion perhaps?"

"Not really. He keeps my mother in a secure suite on the second floor, two bedrooms and a parlor. Someone from the house staff takes food to her three times a day. And I usually check on her at night, and sometimes when she's restless I sleep in the second bedroom."

Simone frowned and scribbled on the tablet again. "You mean secured suite as in *locked*?"

"Yes, he says she's safer that way."

Simone pursed her lips as she considered Victoria's answer. "I guess the next question is how long do you think it'll be before he discovers that you're gone?"

Victoria shrugged. "He's been spending so

much time at work that I don't often see him at home. I know he's planning on personally oversee-ing the videos for the social media ads, which may mean marathon sessions at the office. He keeps a personal suite there, so there's a good chance he'll spend at least one night away, maybe two."

"So, one day, maybe a second, depending on how fast those media ads shape up," Simone surmised.

"I think so," Victoria said in a small not-really-so-sure voice.

"And now, the most important questions of all," Simone warned. "What can you tell us about where the supplement work is done? Where's the lab located? The production facilities? And there's got to be inventory. Where is that kept?"

"It's all at Dragomere Enterprises, in a special off-limits area of the basement. It's all there, and there are guards," Victoria warned.

"Who and how many?"

"A night watchman at the front desk on the main floor. Several of my father's special security people in the basement–"

"People who've been given the supplement?" Simone asked.

"Yes, but I don't know how many would be on duty. Maybe as many as a dozen."

Simone added one last note to the tablet and

etched a couple of heavy lines underneath it before laying down her pen and summarizing the situation for the others. "Our target is that building. And we're going to have to assume we've only got one day to pull things together."

"Are you ready for back-up?" Carter asked.

"We damn sure are," Simone replied, a determined look on her face.

"We need a safe place for everyone to meet," Simone continued. "Someplace secluded but close. Any ideas?"

David raised his hand. "What about the old Deckard acreage?" he asked, referring to a largely ignored plot of packed-dirt flatland outside the city limits that was occasionally used for traveling carnivals.

Heath nodded. "That's perfect. Traffic on that county road is almost non-existent. And when they come, those carnie people bring lots of big rigs and trailers and RVs. There should be plenty of room for your people."

Simone gathered her tablet and pen and stood up. "All right, we've tackled all we can tonight. Victoria, you'll stay here at the safehouse with me. I want the rest of you to go home, get a decent night's sleep. We're going to do our damnedest to pull this off as a covert operation, so try your best to act normal. We don't need a bunch of civilians getting in the way. And we sure don't want Tepesh put on alert. Everyone agreed?

"Good," she said when everyone at the table nodded. "Carter and I will be at the designated camp site in the morning. Join us when you can. I have a feeling it's going to be a hell of a day."

CHAPTER
†
NINETEEN

It took Heath a long time to fall asleep after he snuck back into his family's house that night. Concern over what the next day would bring was definitely one of the issues worrying him, but what had been on his mind more than anything was what Zoe did when he walked her out to her car after the meeting. Instead of their usual quick hug-and-goodbye routine, she'd held on to him longer and tighter than usual, her cheek pressed against his chest. When she'd finally turned her face up to him, he'd seen see the shine of tears in her eyes. She'd whispered, "Promise me you'll be extra, extra careful tomorrow." Then she'd surprised him by tiptoeing up and kissing him. The sweetest kiss he'd ever had.

Later, as he lay alone in his tumbled bed, his

head had been filled with memories. How much a part of his life Zoe was. How he'd always been able to count on her. The fact that she'd been the only one who came to mind the night he so desperately needed help. Why had it taken a disaster to realize how important she was to him, what an important part of his life she was? And how could he make up for it from now on?

$

It was after noon when Heath drove his rental car onto the hard-packed, grassless dirt at the old Deckard farm, eager to search out Zoe and start making up for being such an idiot for so long. The place looked vastly different than it had the one time he'd been there for a carnival.

He pulled into an empty spot next to two good-sized gazebos erected side-by-side near the entrance to the acreage. The flag with a picture of a badger baring its teeth flew above clearly designated the canvas duo as "headquarters." Heath could see Simone and the professor seated just inside at a folding table set up in front of canvas curtains that had been hung to create a back wall of sorts. A small group of tactically clad operatives were gathered round, studying what looked to be copies of Victoria's hand-drawn maps and diagrams.

Victoria sat nearby, obviously on call in case anyone had additional questions about the building that was to be their target.

Another long folding table had been set up under a separate canopy just outside of the main tents and it was loaded with big yellow water barrels, canned soft drinks, plates of ready-made sandwiches, and bowls of apples and oranges for the hungry.

Scattered across the bare ground, Badger members who hadn't already erected their own tents and set out chairs and camp tables were busy doing so. Shaded by a ring of tall trees, the outside perimeter had been turned into a parking area holding several vehicles of various types. Some were battered and well-worn; others were brand new metal beasts with dual-wheels and fancy trappings. A few of the vets had come in SUVs, and one, obviously a free spirit from the 60s or 70s, had come in an old VW panel van, which appeared very discreet and ideal for transporting any type of cargo. The bed of one big pick-up held a large plastic container of liquid and a pump system Heath figured might be gasoline in case anyone needed to refuel. Heath chuckled when he caught sight of the hand-lettered sign reading "restroom this way" with an arrow pointing into the woods that some joker had hung on a tree.

Exiting his car, Heath quickly ducked under the edge of the nearest gazebo. His breath caught in his throat when he noticed another table on the far side of the two joined tents.

Holy crap, this is real, he thought, of suddenly blazingly aware for the first time that all them – his friends and the strangers who'd dropped everything to come and help them. The thought rocked him.

"Hey, have you two seen Zoe around?" Heath asked when the line in front of David dwindled for a minute and his friend finally took notice of him. Carter waved but kept talking to the man in front of him. "I didn't spot her car in the parking area."

"I don't think she's come yet," David answered.

"Really?" Heath said, trying not to show his disappointment. "Oh. Well, her family just recently got back in town. She probably needed to hang around and visit with them for a while."

"Probably," David agreed. A new man walked up, and David went back to work.

"Guess I'll check with Simone, see what she'd like me to do," Heath told them, shoving his hands in his jean pockets and heading for the mob of troopers surrounding the big table where Simone told him to help the two vets manning the weapons table.

Heath wandered over to a patch of shade under one of the trees bordering a row of parked vehicles and found a reasonably comfy seat on a slab of rock half buried in the ground. He'd just downed the last of the can's contents when his cell phone rang. He pulled the device from his back pocket and swiped it open.

"Hello," he greeted, expecting the call to be from his mother, who checked in every few days, but hoping it might be Zoe telling him she was on her way.

"H-Heath?" said a voice made trembly by choked back sobs. "I'm sorry, so sorry. I thought I was going to meet up with you. I didn't know. . . . He t-tricked me."

Heath heard a gasp and then an anguished cry. Fear shot through him and he clasped the phone tighter, pleading, "Zoe, honey, what's going on? Who tricked you? Where are you?"

Heath's stomach did a slow roll when the next voice he heard was male.

"Why, hello, Mr. Harkness. How inconvenient to hear from you again. How lucky for us that my sister didn't do a very good job of hiding her phone before stupidly leaving home. Seeing the log of recent phone calls between you and Victoria, it wasn't too hard to figure out who was causing all our problems, and that conveniently led us to your little friend Zoe. I hope you enjoyed your conversation with her. It's the last one she'll ever have with you or anyone else if you don't crawl back into your miserable little-life shell and keep your nose out of something that's none of your business."

Heath heard Zoe sob louder and then the line was abruptly disconnected. He scrambled to his feet and ran for the main tent. Panicked, he shoved his way through the gaggle of Badger Brigade volunteers at Simone's table, his words tumbling out so fast she had to ask him to repeat what he'd said.

"Oh, hell," she muttered when she finally understood. "Carter," she yelled across the gazebos, "get over here. We've got a whole new problem." Then she turned to Victoria, "We're going to need your input on this."

Heath's frantic arrival and anguished words had put every person in camp on alert. Those not already in the tent gathered quietly around the sides and front, giving the people around Simone's table more space. Murmurs rippled through the crowd as they began to pass on to others what information they could glean from Heath's terrified tale.

"Where would he take her?" Heath pleaded to Victoria. "I've got to do something, stop him from hurting her somehow."

"I know it's difficult, Heath, but you need to calm down," Simone urged. "I know you're scared, and you have a right to be, but if we stand a chance of getting her back, it'll be because we have a better plan than they do."

"You're right," Heath conceded, sucking in a

deep breath. "Just tell me what to do. I've got to go get her."

Victoria swiped away the tears that had begun to fall after hearing Heath's anguished cry for help. "I'm so sorry, Heath. I thought I picked a good place when I hid my phone in my room before I went down to the party. Gregor must still be at the house. I don't see how he could have taken her to work, not in the daytime, not even through the loading dock entrance. It's always crowded with employees who know nothing about what goes on in the basement. He'd feel safer at home where there are security guards."

"I gotta get her out of there," Heath insisted. "Tell me his phone number. I'll call and offer to take her place."

Simone put a restraining hand on his arm. "No, that would be a death sentence for you as well as Zoe. There's no way he'd turn her loose."

"From what you reported about the call – the smug way he taunted you, and the fact that what he said had only to do with you and Zoe – I don't think he has a clue about the coming raid," Professor Stein assured Heath. "That's something in our favor."

"Okay, Victoria, we're back to the main question. Where at the house would he be most likely to keep Zoe?" Carter asked.

"My guess is the extra bedroom in Mother's

rooms. The door to it can be locked as well as the main door to the suite. It would be double secure and out of the way."

It was decided Heath would lead the rescue mission at the Tepesh mansion. Victoria insisted on going with them, stressing the fact that she was the only one who knew exactly where her mother's suite was located and the guards would recognize her.

Stein addressed the group, which included Simone, David, Victoria, and Carter.

"My guess is they're expecting an attack. David, have a drone check out infra-red heat signatures to see how many guards are in the mansion and where. We need some element of surprise; therefore, I'm going to suggest that Victoria and Heath drive up in the van with Carter and a select group of operatives in the back. David can hack the security devices. Carter, do you have any thoughts?"

"I would recommend we split up. My team will secure the area, and I will get Victoria's mom. My operatives can help as needed. This is an extraction operation so we want to leave a small footprint. We'll have small arms with silencers but our primary tools will be pepper-ball guns, smoke bombs, and percussion stun grenades," Carter said.

"Ok, Simone, David and I will stay here and monitor the situation. Good luck people," Stein said.

David launched his first drone.

§

Dragomere felt an enormous amount of satisfaction from his actions. "Gregor, take care of our guest here. I have to leave on business," he said.

"Yes father, I'll just treat her like my sister. Gregor said with a smirk He grabbed Zoe by the upper arm and led her down a dark hallway.

What does he mean, treat me like his sister? What did he do to Victoria? Zoe thought to herself. Gregor quickened his pace. *Oh my God, he raped her.*

He turned her in front of a double door. He turned the knob and flung the door open. Her breathing had increased from her recent realization. He marched her over to a king-sized bed and slapped her so hard that she flew in the air before bouncing on the bed. She was almost unconscious as Gregor climbed on top of her. In one swift move he ripped open her blouse.

"Wait. Can't we kiss for a while?" she asked.

Puzzled, Gregor bent over to comply. She put both her hands on his face, leaned in, and then clamped down as hard as she could with her teeth on his nose. Instinctively, Gregor pushed her away so hard her petite body bounced on the bed. She caught herself and rolled off the bed and made a dash for the door. Gregor, holding his nose, chased after her.

David successfully breached the mansion's cyber defenses and took control. His drone spotted the guard's locations on the premises. The security cameras revealed the bulk of the guards in the basement by the lab.

The van slowly entered the front gate. A red curtain separated Heath and Victoria from the rest of the van hiding Carter and his team.

"I'm picking up two people running in the central hallway." David's voice rang through the team's ear pieces. Heath became noticeably aggravated.

Zoe was lost. She needed to run. She frantically turned a corner, saw an open door, and ducked in. Within seconds she heard Gregor whiz by. She purveyed the area. It was a ballroom. She saw a bar at the end of the room and ran toward it. She knew she couldn't hide for long so she looked for an overproof liquor. A bottle of 151 proof answered her call. She poured the contents into a glass, spilling some on the bar. She feverishly looked for a lighter and hopefully a cigarette. Come on, you're a bartender; you have to have a pack of smokes lying around, she thought. Then she saw it.

Gregor burst into the room.

"Well, look who showed up," said the sentry at the gate. "Oh, and you brought a little playmate."

Victoria lowered the van window and shot the guard in the face with a pepper ball. Heath jumped out and opened the back of the van. Carter and his team spread out to secure the perimeter, with one operative tying up the sentry and dragging him off to his guard shack.

Zoe lit the cigarette and grabbed the drink. Gregor raced toward the bar. The cigarette dangled from her lips.

"Having one last drink?" Gregor said.

"No. You are," she said as she splashed the booze on Gregor's face and flicked the cigarette at him, creating a small fireball.

Gregor grabbed his face and tried to rub the liquid off. Zoe saw her chance and made a dash for the door.

She ran into the study and tried to open the window to escape into the courtyard.

"Zoe!" Heath shouted from the hallway.

As she heard his voice, she was overcome by a wave of relief.

"I'm in the study, Heath!"

Within seconds Heath appeared. He saw her by the window with her blouse torn and bra showing.

Before he could get angry, he felt a thud to the back of his head, knocking him down.

"Well, if it isn't Heath Harkness," Gregor said. "Looks like my men screwed up. No matter, you won't leave here alive, and then I can get back to having some fun."

Heath rolled over. Gregor moved to crush Heath with his foot. Heath quickly redirected Gregor's foot, causing him to stumble backwards. Heath jumped up and ran at Gregor.

"This way," Victoria said.

Carter followed her up the stairs to the second floor. Before they reached the top, Carter grabbed her arm and slowed her down. He put his finger to his lips to signal silence. Carter bobbed his head up to see two guards in front of the furthest hallway door.

"Get ready," he whispered. Carter sprang from the stairwell and fired multiple pepper-ball shots at the two men. He knocked one out and struck the other one in the groin. He quickly disarmed them.

"Stand back," he said as he raised his leg to kick the door in.

Zoe heard a couple shots ring out and quickly moved from the window. She spied a mahogany and oak desk in the corner of the room and ducked underneath it only raising her head to see how Heath was doing.

While Heath's martial skill was superior, it seemed the blows and throws had little impact on Gregor, who kept fighting like a well-oiled machine. All of a sudden Gregor grabbed Heath, picked him up, and threw him in Zoe's direction. She automatically ducked as Heath's body struck the massive desk. He hit with such force it knocked open all the drawers and sent Zoe flying to the ground.

Once Zoe got back up, she saw what appeared to be a black handle of a knife. The blade was silver, shiny, and sharp with some words scribbled across it, which she could not read. In the middle of the handle was a silver eagle holding a swastika. On top of the handle was the insignia of the SS. Lying underneath the knife was a black and white autographed picture. She picked up the knife, removed it from its sheath, and put it behind her. The photograph was of Adolf Hitler. A chill ran through her body.

Gregor grabbed Heath by the throat with one hand and lifted him up in the air. He saw Zoe by his father's desk and moved toward her, holding Heath's body. Slamming Heath onto the desk, Gregor fixed both hands around his throat and began to squeeze. Heath grabbed Gregor's wrists and tried to loosen the grip but to no avail. Gregor smiled at Zoe to intimidate her and opened his mouth to reveal his growing fangs.

Zoe stood motionless as she saw Heath begin to lose his energy. In a flash of absolute anger, she plunged the dagger into Gregor's right eye. The sheer pain of the silver knife entering his brain made Gregor jump back. He screamed as he wrapped his hands around the bleeding wound.

With Gregor now facing him, Heath delivered a strong, step-side kick that launched Gregor some twenty feet in the air, causing him to land in the large fireplace with such force as to break the controls and ignite the flames. Screaming in agony, Gregor rolled off the logs and onto the floor, quickly to try to put out the fire engulfing his body.

Heath moved toward Gregor to finish him off but was intercepted by Zoe. "Let's get the hell out of here."

Heath nodded, and they both left to look for Victoria and Carter.

"Freeze," came the voice over Carter's com unit. "My drone sees a guy pointing a gun at the mom's head. He is standing in back of her. If you break the door, she's dead."

"We need a distraction," Carter said. "David, is there anything you can do with that drone?"

"Yes. There's a window in back of him. I can smash the drone into it, but it's 50/50 if it works."

"Do it. We have no other choice." Carter said as he drew his 10mm with an attached silencer.

As David yelled "Now," Carter crashed in the door. As the guard turned back around, his chest was met with a bullet, which threw him back. Carter could see he had a bulletproof vest on so he let another round fly into his head, causing the guard to spin to the ground.

Victoria launched toward her mother, who greeted her with open arms. Heath and Zoe entered the room.

"The first floor is clear for now," Heath said.

"Did you run into Gregor?" Carter asked.

"Yeah. He's smoking." Zoe replied.

"You could say he made an ash of himself." Heath said.

Then Zoe saw Victoria and her eyes teared up. Both women hugged.

"Come on people, we got to move," Carter said.

With that command the team ran outside, scrambled back into the van, and peeled out.

§

Once back at the base the team met with Stein

and the rest of the group. Hugs and handshakes permeated the reunion.

"What do you think will happen next?" Heath asked.

"Well, I don't think we're going to see this on the news," Stein said.

Simone's cell phone pinged. She opened it up. It was a text from one of her operatives, which said, "Quick, take a look at this. I just got it."

She started watching the video, then paused it. She turned to the group. "Here. This is Tepesh's speech at the Platinum Club. Take a look, guys."

Part of the wall by the large painting of Dragomere opened, and Dragomere moved into the room. He looked around. All the people he had invited were there. He smiled and gave a nod in the direction of Gregor, who moved to the head of the table and began to speak.

"Friends, patriots, welcome. We have been on a long journey to secure what is rightfully ours. Tonight our victory begins."

The crowd cheered.

"For too long we had to suffer while the lazy takers stole our profits, but no more," Gregor said as he raised his fist toward the ceiling. More cheers came from the audience.

"Tonight my father will enlighten you with our

plan that will change your future forever. Please welcome him."

As more claps came from the crowd, Gregor shook his father's hand and moved away from the table. Dragomere took a slow look around the table and began to speak with a slight hint of a foreign accent.

"Tonight marks the dawning of a new day, a day for those captains of industry to regain their proper position in society and in the world. Tonight I will lay out my plan and how to accomplish it. You already know the commitment that I need from you."

"Yeah and it's a hell of a lot of money, Dragomere. Close to a trillion dollars. What the hell are you going to do with it?" Volch asked.

"Well, Mr. Volch. I know you and your brother have been very active in our cause to elect the right type of people," Dragomere said. This investment will secure the presidency for us. Plus, as an investment of stock in my company, it is washed clean from government intrusion and will allow me, using my bank, to borrow as much money as necessary to insure we get our man in the White House."

"Dragomere, so far 'our' man is losing by more than fifteen points. We have been very generous in supporting you, and you know that, but we're losing. What are you going to do to fix this?" Volch said.

"You will see tonight," Dragomere said as he

motioned to the boardroom door, which swung open. Governor Walters walked in. The governor waved his hand to say hello. Some of the guests applauded while others remained silent. The governor sat at the head of the long, dark cherry-wood boardroom table.

"I know what you are thinking. Really, I do," said Dragomere. "Let me tell you why the governor will win. It is because the American people still believe in miracles, that's how. But let me finish my speech first. Let me show you how I will triple your investment. Here are my ten points of freedom.

"First, we will abolish abortion." The crowd cheers. "Once we stack the Supreme Court, we'll have one of the backward states that we own put forth a law making abortion illegal after six weeks. This will give our base what they want, which is more control over women," Tepesh said.

"Second, total privatization of schools to produce students that just follow orders so they can be easily indoctrinated into the workforce without protesting for a higher minimum wage. We've been rather successful with this plan in Britain and Mexico. In fact, in the US it is likely we can eliminate the minimum wage. It's just a simple step after we eliminate the prevailing wage.

"Third, we will legislate more austerity measures. We've got a number of countries already under our control by doing this, and it is proving rather successful for us.

"Fourth, we'll have more voter suppression laws. Hopefully, with our gerrymandering we'll have our legislators pass laws that will allow them to void any election where they feel there was anything illegal going on, which will help our candidates get elected. This, of course, with removing early voting, drive through voting, absentee voting, and using the crosscheck system, will keep us in power.

"Fifth we want a tougher stance on crime especially on drug crime. This will boost profits in the private prisons business. No legalization of pot – ever.

"Sixth, as part of a tough-on-crimes initiative, we'll pass a law that says felons can be hired for less than minimum wage, which will eventually make them work for free. We will create more debtors prisons. These prisoners can then be purchased by corporations and allow individuals in those prisons to work as slaves. This is how we'll bring back slavery. Can't pay back your student loan? Then you will work for free.

"Seventh, we will eliminate the unions and everything they and that socialist FDR brought that minimized our profits."

"That's brilliant, Dragomere," one of the guests said.

The speech was broken up by more clapping. Tepesh held his hand up to quiet the audience.

"Eighth, we're going to expand wolf and other animal hunting and contests here and in other parts of the country. In fact, for Wisconsin, I'm going to make sure that this includes hunting pregnant wolves with dogs. Then I'm going to make the taxpayer pay a few thousand dollars for any injured or dead hunting dog. Of course, they won't have to verify anything, just submit a claim. Oh, and we'll go over the DNR quota too. It will be a nice gift to our friends and supporters, especially in Wisconsin. Face it, no one cares about protecting wolves, and our supporters do so love to gut shoot them."

"Wait a minute. This is only going to work if we retain the governorship," said Mrs. Henderson.

"No," Tepesh quickly said. "If for some reason we lose the governorship, we control the Assembly and the Senate, so before the governor leaves, he'll sign a law severely handicapping the new governor from doing anything. Then we'll wage a political campaign bashing him for failing to do anything. What is the governor going to do? Take it to the State Supreme Court? We own that too. We've done this before, and it works like a charm."

Tepesh looked around the room and saw that people were starting to get bored.

"I will tell you more but let me cut to the reason

you are here. As I was saying, to all of you who care to finally take our place in history, I promise you immortality."

At first the room was quiet. The guests looked in amazement at one another. Then the murmurings began. "I know you're skeptical but have you not all tried my super steroid? Did it not work wonders for you?" Tepesh asked.

"Yes. I know I feel younger and can accomplish more," a guest said.

"Especially with your girlfriends," Tepesh said.

The crowd laughed.

"My guess is you'd like some proof. Governor, have you had the opportunity to take the dark red pill I gave you last week?"

"Yes, I took it last Wednesday," he said.

"Excellent. Now Governor, perhaps you can tell these fine people how you are feeling right now."

"Well. I feel . . ."

The bullet from Tepesh's derringer splattered the front of the governor's forehead, along with brain matter, on the white linen tablecloth in front of the guests. Shock and horror filled the room. Suddenly, more of Tepesh's security personnel in their black paramilitary uniforms and assault rifles began to fill the room. Guests stood with the shock of seeing someone murdered in front of their eyes.

"Sit down, everyone," Tepesh said, waving his

pistol in the air. "Now. Wait." Tepesh pointed to the governor's lifeless body.

The crowd reluctantly sat down. They watched the governor. Suddenly, his left outstretched arm shook. As he raised his head from the table, his skull began to heal over his new-grown brain matter. His other arm started to shake and then his body. His head was now banging on the table, the skull all healed up, and even the hair had started to grow back in the affected area.

Jack was astounded. This event was nothing he was prepared for.

With his head upright, Todd Walters sat up and looked around.

"What is all this blood and pink macaroni in front of me?" he asked.

"It's just your brain. Tell me, how do you feel?" Tepesh asked.

"Um, fine. I guess. In fact, I feel different. I can breathe better, and wow, the colors are clearer. I feel stronger," Walters said as he touched his head gingerly. Walters grabbed a nearby candle holder and bent it in half with ease.

"This is incredible. I feel like, like, like . . ."

"A God." Tepesh finished the governor's sentence.

"All of you can be like this." Tepesh said. "You can be immortal. All it takes to finish the treatment is this dark red pill."

Tepesh held up the small capsule in front of them.

"You want to know how we're going to win this election. This is how. Most of the electorate still believe in miracles. When the governor here gives his next speech, a shot will ring out. He'll go down. He'll be pronounced dead and then all of a sudden he will rise from the dead. 'It's a miracle!' America will chant."

Tepesh raised his hands above his head."Who would question the work of God?"

The crowd stood up and applauded him. Tepesh stepped behind the governor and placed his hand on the governor's shoulder.

"Ladies and gentlemen. My son will be placing contracts in front of you. This is your one and only chance to become part of history, to live forever. The contract calls for an investment of a percentage of your net worth. Specifically, given your current financial situation, I have estimated the correct sum from each of you. Roughly, all of you together will be providing me with about twenty-eight billion dollars. A small price to pay for immortality. The contract also states that you will not try to duplicate this formula. Now ladies and gentlemen, what is your answer?" Tepesh shouted as he raised his hands toward the roof.

The crowd responded with more applause. Tepesh appeared to gloat at his admiring audience.

"Impressive, but what are you going to do about that reporter that's hounding you. That Jack Stein?" Mrs. Henderson asked.

"Oh please, I'm way ahead of you." Tepesh said. "He is of no consequence. I'm one step ahead of everyone."

Simone turned off the video. "This is what we're up against," she said.

"Holly crap," Carter said.

"I knew it. He developed the immortality drug," Stein said

He goes on to brag more about the same old stuff his political party has been spouting, but he knows." Simone said.

"If this is true, how does he know?" Stein said.

"Who would have known? My security was tight," Carter said.

Stein looked to his comrades and said, "We have to be very vigilant from now on."

"Where did you come from?" Stein asked.

"I have something to tell you. Can we talk in private?" Heath asked Stein.

"Sure," Stein said as the two walked away from

the group. Heath filled him in on what happened to his body since being drowned in the lake.

At Stein's request Heath agreed to see Dr. Caroline Yang, the head of the school nursing department, the next night.

§

Fall made its appearance known through the brisk night air. Heath contemplated his life with some foreboding. He walked down the stairs to the nursing school and into the bowels of the college, passing large, old portraits of the previous presidents of the college. Heath could smell an age-old musk that permeated the hallway. As he walked he felt Zoe's warm hand envelop his. He looked at her and smiled. She smiled back.

The sign on the double glass doors read Health Sciences. Heath looked forward and he could see the doctor running toward him. She reached the door and unlocked it.

"Sorry about that. We usually keep it locked," she said, barely taking her eyes off of Heath.

"Jack filled me in on what happened to you. It's very strange," she said as they reached the lab. "Here, have a seat and take off your shirt." She motioned for him to sit. "Let's start with blood pressure." The doctor rolled a blood pressure cuff on Heath's arm and pumped away as her eyes grew wider and wider. She paused.

"Very little blood pressure?" she said.

"So I am dead?" Heath said.

"Hang on. Let me try something."

She tried the cuff again and for a longer time period. She looked at the instrument and then at Heath. "Well, you're technically not dead as you do have a pulse, but it's so low it's barely noticeable. On the other hand you're not exactly human. Do you have any aches or pains?"

"No. Not really. Well, when I'm in direct sunlight, I feel a little faint, otherwise I feel really good. I don't feel hungry like I once did, and I'm craving almost raw type meat. I seem to run faster without even getting tired. I'm not sleeping that well. And I want to sleep during the day. Have you ever heard of anything like this?

"I have heard a little about this, and it's been associated with a supplement that the Tepesh scientists have been working on," she said as she went to look for an article. She went to a stack of papers and began moving them around.

"Ouch." She raised a finger, cut by a piece of paper. She instinctively squeezed it and was going to wash it off when she saw Heath glaring at her. "Heath, what's on your mind?"

"I don't know but it's like I want to taste that blood."

"Hang on a minute," she said as she washed her finger and bandaged it. She went over to a large refrigerator and pulled out a pint of blood. She opened the container and poured a little blood, filling a tablespoon. "Heath, I would like you to smell this blood," she said as she walked toward him.

Suddenly, when she was a foot away, she saw his body change. It became more muscular. She lifted the spoon to his nose, and in less than a second, Heath swallowed the blood.

"I told you just to smell it."

"I'm sorry. It's like I had no control."

Dr. Yang looked concerned. She then noticed something strange around his lips. "Can you open your mouth, please."

Heath obliged, and Dr. Yang noticed two sharp fangs growing in the top row of his teeth. "What's going on in your body right now?"

"It's like my senses are heightened. I have this weird feeling we are being spied on," Heath said.

"There is no one here but us," said the doctor.

Heath turned his head to the left and saw a large moth perched on a wall. He unhooked himself from the blood pressure cuff and slowly walked toward it. He was a few yards away when the moth took flight, heading toward the ceiling. Within a second Heath was air bound and grabbed the moth. He threw it on a table on his way down and shattered it, with tiny pieces of metal and plastic flying all over the surface.

"It's a spy drone," Heath said. He began to gather the pieces. "I think professor Stein will want to see this."

"True, but let's finish testing you first."

She led him through a series of movements, measuring his strength, speed and agility.

"When did you first start feeling different and able to do these things? she asked.

"It was after I was thrown in the lake. First, I thought I had drowned, but then it was like something kicked in and I felt a lot of energy. It felt like an explosion in my body, uniting it. I swam like crazy out of the lake and I'm not a great swimmer. Also, just right now, when I drank the blood, I had a download of information going into my brain. It was medical stuff and ancient acupuncture stuff. I can name all of these medical instruments," he said, pointing to the metal tray sitting next to Dr. Yang that was filled with different instruments.

Dr. Yang's eyes widened. "Before I got my MD I got a Phd in acupuncture, but almost no one knows that. The blood I gave you was mine. My knowledge just transferred to you through my blood."

"From what I heard, the Tepesh people have

been working on some type of super anti-aging supplement," he said as he reached in his jeans and pulled out a dark red pill. "Victoria gave this to me." he said. He handed the pill over to the doctor. "I'm wondering if there is a way to reverse engineer it and make it harmful to those that are on it?

"That's exactly what I was thinking," she said. "The bottomline on the results of your exam is that whatever happened to you has put your body in a state of flux. I can't say, based on what I found, that you meet the definition of a human being all the time. Overall, you have very low blood pressure, but you are functioning at a higher level than most humans. Your skills are at Olympic-athlete levels. However, when you ingest blood, your powers increase beyond normal human levels. Historically, the Nazis experimented with creating super soldiers, and then after the war, those doctors went to work for us. The twist here is that some of them discovered a formula that has a disastrous side effect. Either you need a steady supply of pills or you have to access human blood."

"So you're telling me I'm a cross between Captain America and Dracula?" Heath said.

"I hate to put it that way but yes."

"Can you cure me?"

"I don't know, but I'm going to try," she said.

"I'll take some of your blood and do some more tests on it, but we're done with the physical exam.

"Can I share this info with Professor Stein and others as necessary?" she asked.

"Yes, of course.

"Here is some paperwork for you to sign to allow me to do that."

"Thank you," Heath said as he signed the document.

The doctor took Heath's blood, then thanked him for coming.

As Heath left, Dr. Yang phoned Professor Stein.

"Hi, Jack, this is Caroline. You were right. Heath's athletic ability tested off the charts and may change in relation to the ingestion of blood or super steroid. To what point, I can't be sure. He also has the ability to download people's knowledge and abilities based on ingesting a tablespoon of blood, but I don't know how long that lasts. I saw him jump up about five feet to catch a drone moth."

"A what?" Stein asked.

"Heath promised to get what's left of it to you," she said.

"Spy drone. Well, that explains a lot," he said.

"So we don't fully know the extent of his powers then?"

"Correct."

"Have you ever encountered anything like this before?" he asked.

"Not personally, but my ancestry is full of stories of Qigong, Kung Fu and Tai Chi masters doing extraordinary things, from levitating to throwing people around with energy and absorbing blows without injury. My guess is that somehow he is able to access the pineal gland, also known as the third eye. That's where all these powers manifest. Normally, have taken masters and sages years of training and meditation to access this."

"Thank you. I appreciate your help."

"You're most welcome."

CHAPTER
†
TWENTY

The January evening was a balmy sixty-four degrees in New Orleans as the caravan of black secret-service SUVs made their way to the parking lot in back of Tepesh's orphanage. The front was besieged by a bevy of limos dropping off the Tepesh tux-clad supporters and Walters backers. The scene was observed by Simone sitting outside a coffee shop a few blocks away. She texted Stein that the last limo had dropped off its guests. Now came the waiting game. Stein would give an appropriate amount of time for everyone to settle in. The uninvited and reconstructed insect drone found its perch on an old ceiling beam in the ballroom where the event was supposed to take place. As the drone notified the group that the introductions were about to begin, the van dropped Stein off down the block and proceeded to its designation.

Stein exited the van. He took in a slow breath, realizing he might be killed, and with conviction he took his first step toward the building. Memories of Simone and the times they shared filled his head. He turned the corner and saw the two guards in front of the orphanage. Nonchalantly, he stepped toward them. They gripped their AR-15s tighter.

"Hello. I'm expected. My name is Jack Stein."

One brute mumbled something into his sleeve and then said, "Wait here."

Stein didn't have to wait too long. One guard motioned him to enter as the other one opened the door. He stepped into the old musty building that was built in the nineteen twenties. The guard motioned him forward, and Stein proceeded on the well-worn carpet runner. They passed a number of offices and came to a wooden spiral staircase.

"Follow the stairs and security will let you in," the guard said.

Stein made his way up, and one guard opened the door. As he stepped in, Stein saw a sea of tuxes and diamond-studded gowns that made him feel like he stepped back into the gilded age where the middle class did not exist, which he recognized was Tepesh's plan. He felt self-conscious yet proud as the only one wearing a suit. He scouted the area for Tepesh.

Suddenly, the lights began to dim in the ballroom. A spotlight struck the podium on the stage, which was elevated six feet above the ballroom floor. Slowly, the boney fingers of Dragomere Tepesh crossed the beam of light to possess the podium. He was outfitted in a tuxedo with tails and draped in a black cape that had a silky red lining.

"Ladies and gentlemen, welcome to our celebration. We now own the Whitehouse, the Senate, Congress, and the Supreme Court. Soon we will stack all the lower courts with our people and control America. It took thirty years to start to reverse the policies of that wealth-traitor and socialist FDR but we've done it. And thanks to all the media outlets we control, we have influenced enough people to take charge once again. No more middle class," Tepesh said. His grin ran across his face as he surveyed the audience back and forth.

"Lights," he said. Then all the lights in the room came on.

"Ladies and gentlemen, it appears our victory is not quite a hundred percent complete. We have with us Mr. Jack Stein, formerly of the New York Times and now an intellectual elitist college professor and defender of the poor and downtrodden." Tepesh pointed to Stein as the audience booed. The eyes of the crowd leered at Stein as those near him moved away. "So, Mr. Stein, have you come here to save America and the middle class then?"

"That is the plan," Stein said.

"You know you can never defeat the rich. Especially now with the Citizens United decision that allows us to pour millions into political campaigns and bribe politicians legally. And we own every office. What are you going to do?" Tepesh said.

"You forgot to mention voter suppression, gerrymandering, and the crosscheck system," Stein said. "You know if you have to do all that, your ideas suck to the American people and they don't want them."

Tepesh raised his voice. "Give me a large majority of all the radio stations and I'll tell them what to want. We've been influencing the American people since Reagan said he wouldn't enforce the Fairness Doctrine. In other countries they have a practice of killing journalists. Perhaps that should be our next goal. We have enough agents in military and law enforcement positions already."

"Is that what you plan to do to me?" Stein said.

"Kill you? Yes, it is. You will be taken to the basement where you will be drained of blood, slowly and painfully. Then your blood will be shared with our guests."

"Even the President will drink my blood?" Stein asked.

"Yes, of course he will. No one will stop us now," Tepesh said.

"Guards, assist Mr. Stein downstairs."

"I'll stop you," Stein said. "You are not going to win this one, Tepesh. The people are waking up. They know the system is rigged to favor the rich. They will stand up to you and your minions."

The red velvet curtain on the stage swooshed as President Walters entered and stood next to Tepesh. "How are you going to do that?" Walters asked Stein.

"I'm going to go to that fire alarm and press it."

A commotion erupted among the guests as they started to get up from their tables.

"Sit down," Tepesh yelled.

"You and your little band of socialists have lost, Jack," Walters said.

"Bite me," said Stein.

Walters flew into a rage and jumped off the stage, scaring his secret service detail, who followed immediately. Walters grabbed the lapels of Stein's jacket and lifted him in the air while he opened his mouth to reveal two large fangs. Two secret service agents grabbed Walters arms and tried to release Stein. With one swat of Walter's arm, he sent an agent flying onto a dining table, sending it crashing to the ground, causing some guests to fall over.

"Put him down," Tepesh yelled.

Walters reluctantly set Stein down and stepped several feet back.

"Now, Mr. Stein was going to show how he's

going to stop us. Go ahead, Mr. Stein, pull the fire alarm," Tepesh said.

Stein slowly walked from the middle of the ballroom to the fire alarm on the wall and activated it. The sound echoed through the building. Stein looked up at the ceiling, perplexed as he walked back to the center of the room.

Tepesh grinned. "You look surprised. Yes, I found your little lighting system that would shoot a form of hyper-potent light that would kill anyone who took the super supplement or drank blood. I took it apart. As usual, I'm several steps ahead of you. Pity, you lose again."

"Oh, I don't think so," Stein said with a grin.

§

The doctor and two nurses, hearing the fire alarm go off and without receiving any countermanding instruction, began to evacuate the basement with the orphans in tow. As procedure dictated, they marched toward the end of the block. Within seconds one van pulled up in front of them and one in back. The vans' doors swung open and Simone yelled, "Children get in. We'll drive you to safety."

The children quickly ran to the closest van. The doctor grabbed the arm of a small girl, who screamed for help. In a second Heath flew out the door and grabbed the doctor by the neck in mid-air before throwing him several feet into a nearby garden. He picked up the girl, who hugged his neck tightly, and ran into the closest van. Once in the van, the children were driven to a safehouse. The guards at the front of the orphanage watched this transpire, but they were under orders not to leave their post, so did nothing.

§

What's so funny, Mr. Stein?" Tepesh asked.

"I believe dinner has just left the building," Stein said.

Tepesh then realized he didn't tell the doctor to stay put and disregard the fire alarm. Tepesh became enraged and jumped off the stage, heading toward Stein like a torpedo. Walters thrust his hand out in front of Tepesh. "Wait. Let me kill him."

"No. He's mine. Dinner has not left the building. I'm staring at it," Tepesh said.

"Activate," Stein said.

Within a second the sprinkler system installed on the ceiling became active, spewing a reddish colored liquid meant to kill all those that had been exposed to the super supplement or who drank blood.

Walters let out a blood-curdling scream as he looked up to see what was going on and got hit full force with the shower of formula. He fell to his knees, still screaming in pain. The secret service agents were not affected and grabbed him by both arms and tried to drag him from the room. His body began to writhe like that of a fish out of water, and the agents could no longer hang onto him. His face developed large pustules, which then exploded with blood and puss. Walters finally steadied himself and stretched his hand out to a nearby agent, who grabbed it and tried to pull the screaming Walters to a side door. After a few feet the fleshy hand melted in the agent's hand, leaving remnants of bone.

Tepesh, feeling pain for the first time in decades, raised his cape to cover his head and ran out the side door and down the steps. Patrons of the event weren't so lucky. Neither were Tepesh's guards, who were on the drug. Moans and screams filled the room as the desperate tried to break through the locked, double doors with no avail. Some expired on the floor with their flesh separating itself from their bodies and blood pouring onto the old, dry wooden floor.

Tepesh jumped from the stairs and landed in the cobblestone alley separating the church from the orphanage. Stone-faced gargoyles looked down on the scene. He wiped the small drizzles of blood from his face and proceeded to walk toward the parking lot. A red van pulled up in front of him, blocking his exit. Heath opened the door and stepped out. Tepesh could see Victoria was driving and froze in his tracks.

"Heath Harkness, you ignorant peasant, how dare you interfere with my plans. It will be my pleasure to squeeze your neck till your head falls off.

"You attacked my country, my state, my friends, and my life. Time for you to taste some justice, you racist Nazi," said Heath.

The two ran at each other. Tepesh sidestepped Heath's attack. Tearing his cape off, he threw it around Heath's face and slammed him into the brick wall with such force he indented it. Heath threw the cape off and headed toward Tepesh, who threw a right hook that Heath easily ducked under. Heath punched Tepesh so hard in the mouth it sounded like a thunderclap and sent Tepesh flying several feet. Tepesh touched his split lip. Like a cobra, Tepesh responded with lightning speed, attacking Heath, who countered most every blow and returned them with equal ferocity. The scene looked like something out of a matrix movie. In a surprise move, Tepesh feigned a punch and bent down, tackling Heath by the waist and smashing him into the wall. Then he reached up and grabbed Heath by the throat and began to squeeze, lifting him up against the wall. Heath grabbed Tepesh's wrist and then sliding his other hand unto Tepesh's forehead, moved his fingers down and into Tepesh's eyes, forcing him back several feet.

Heath then yelled, "Victoria, he's too strong. I need those pills."

Victoria reached into her coat and pulled out a plastic bag containing six dark red pills and threw them towards Heath. Tepesh jumped and grabbed them before they could reach their destination.

Creating some distance between himself and Heath, he said, "You fools. Now you can die together."

"You'd kill your own daughter?" Heath said.

Tepesh smiled. "She's not my daughter. My chief of security got seduced by your mother in her attempt to get away from me. She didn't succeed and he became dinner. The only good thing your mother ever did was to convince me not to sell you into sex slavery but marry you off to someone wealthy."

Victoria's face expressed shock and happiness simultaneously.

As the sirens of the fire engine became apparent, Tepesh knew he had to finish the job quickly and popped all the super steroids into his mouth. Heath smiled, and Victoria joined him.

Tepesh looked puzzled, but he didn't have long to wait for an explanation, as immense pain erupted in Tepesh's stomach, and he doubled over and screamed. He lifted his head slightly, looking at the two of them.

"Those weren't your precious little super-steroids," Victoria said. "We created a formula that kills the effect of those steroids and for anyone that drank human blood. You just swallowed six times the regular dose, you misogynistic, racist Nazi pig."

With the last ounce of anger in his body, he grabbed Victoria by the upper arms and tried to bite her neck. Before he could lower his fangs on to her alabaster neck, a strong arm snaked in around his throat and moved him backwards. Victoria reached under her coat and pulled out a six-inch silver dagger. She sped toward Tepesh and plunged the knife deep into his chest, turned it, and withdrew it, causing a torrent of blood to spew forth.

"Mother wanted you to have this," she said.

As Heath increased pressure on the rear choke, Tepesh's left eye fell out, rolled down his cheek, and splattered onto the street. At the same time, Heath felt Tepesh's neck snap and his body go limp. Heath released the body, which flopped on the ground and began aging rapidly until all that was left was a steaming slurpy of flesh and bone. The bones then began to disintegrate and decompose rapidly, eventually turning to an ash like substance.

"Hey, get this van out of here," a fireman yelled.

This woke Heath and Victoria from their daze. "Right away," said Heath.

Victoria jumped in the driver's seat as Heath closed his door. She calmly drove away, heading to the safehouse they were staying at.

EPILOGUE

Legal representation was waiting for Stein when he reached the local FBI office in the form of Simone. The FBI could not make a case of murder as there was nothing lethal in the sprinkler system to kill a human being. Footage obtained from the drone showed that both Walters and Tepesh threatened to kill Stein and feed him to the guests, making them all accomplices to murder. This justified a self-defense plea on behalf of Stein. In the end they knew the Justice Department could not make any charge stick, especially after the testimony of the rescued orphans. For the FBI to even come close to a charge would mean they would have to believe Tepesh was a vampire as well as the president. Something they would not wish to consider doing.

The orphans were sworn to secrecy so no one ever would find out about Victoria's, Heath's, or Zoe's involvement.

Once back at Parkwood, Heath and Victoria faced a bittersweet goodbye. The third-floor cafeteria overlooked a small, wooded park next to a small frozen lake. The sun was bright but Heath sat at the table that had the shade pulled down.

"Trying to get yourself acclimated?" Victoria said.

"Something like that," Heath said.

Victoria sat down in from of him. After a quiet interlude, Heath spoke.

"So this is goodbye?"

"Yes, I'm afraid it has to be. Gregor is a wanted man for his role in the immortality plot, plus countless other crimes. Simone has gathered a legal team for me to fight to be the sole heir to the Tepesh estate. I have responsibilities to right the wrongs my family caused the world."

She reached over and grabbed Heath's hand. "You will, however, always have a special place in my heart," she said.

"And you in mine," he said.

They both looked over and saw Zoe approaching.

"I think that's my cue," she said. "You're in good hands."

Victoria stood up and, approaching Zoe, gave her a hug, which was reciprocated.

"I'll miss you. It will be kind of dull here without you," Zoe said.

"I'll miss you too, although I think Heath may have a few ideas," Victoria said.

Heath went over by the couple, and they all hugged each other one final time.

§

The sun bounced off the green and white striped tent of Cafe Du Monde as Professor Stein enjoyed a cup of French roast coffee on a brisk Monday morning. He noticed Simone snaking her way through the tourists that traditionally occupied that area of New Orleans.

"What, no beignets?" Simone said.

Stein smiled. "I'm trying to cut down on the sweets."

The waiter came over and offered some coffee, which Simone gleefully accepted.

"So now what are you going to do, Jack?" Simone asked.

"Good question. Frankly, I didn't think destroying Tepesh and his immortality plot would be this easy to walk away from without any form of punishment. I spent the weekend in jail, but outside of a fine for turning on the fire alarm, there was nothing. I mean we broke in and altered the sprinkler system."

"True, but they would have to prove that and

given it saved orphans, who would want to charge you? Plus, you're a white male and can get away with murder as long as you use the privilege words of self-defense," she said.

"Well, that's certainly and unfortunately true," he said. "Good point. There also haven't been any leaks to the media, which is strange. The official story, which came from Walter's PAC, said he died of a heart attack and the guests died of food poisoning. They are, of course, suggesting it was a plot by the opposing party. Anyway, I'm not going to worry about it. Classes start next week, although I could easily get replacements and move back to Manhattan."

"True, but come on, Jack, you know you love Madison. You can live there and still drive to the college, or you could teach at UW Madison," she said.

"Or I could stay in Madison and write a screen-play about this. Fiction, of course. I wonder if George Clooney might be interested in playing me?" Stein said.

"I was thinking Liev Schreiber might be a better match."

"I could see that too.

"What's next for you?" he asked.

"I have some catching up to do. We have a new president, I need to do a deeper dive into his background," she said.

"Ah, yes, Roland Klumpf, another oligarch who got his money by inheriting it. From what I heard, the guy is a real clown. No one takes him seriously. He's in debt. He can't seem to go beyond rightwing talk channels. And I think he has some holdings in reality shows, porn, and real estate," Stein said.

"Remember, they thought Hitler was a clown too. This isn't about elections anymore. It's about the control of America by the fascists in any way possible, whether through voter suppression, gerrymandering, or even an insurrection, if necessary. Thirty years have been spent in loosening gun laws to make it easy for these militias to organize, train, and intimidate. Once the call is given, they will be ready. Will we?" she said.

"Looks like Madison, here I come. Oh, do you remember the name of Klumpf's business?"

After pausing to think a bit, she said, "Orange King Enterprises."

Acknowledgment

I would like to thank Laurie Scheer and Christine Desmet of the UW Madison Writer's Institute for getting me on the "write" path. Kira Henschel of Henshel Haus Publishing for guidance publishing my first works. LaRee Bryant for her editorial acumen and work on this project. Finally, thanks to Christine Keleny of CKBooks Publishing for turning my words into actions.

Author Biography

Wes Manko has incorporated his eighteen-plus years of teaching Systema – Russian Martial Art and woman's self-defense with an academic background consisting of college degrees in Police Science and Criminal Justice, along with a master's degree in Public Administration into making the public aware of how violence can be prevented. He has taught at Marquette University, University of Milwaukee, and Mount Mary university. Through his business, DEFENSEWORKS, he provided training to corporations, non-profit organizations, individuals, and military and law enforcement personnel. In 2005 he received a citation from the Wisconsin State Assembly for his work.

He entered the writing arena in 1996 when his article on preventing violence at work became the cover story for City Edition, a Milwaukee news publication. Since then his articles have been published in several national publications including *Black Belt Magazine*. His books include *Color Me Safe: A Woman's Self-Defense Coloring Book* by HenschelHaus Publishing in 2018. *Your Best Defense: Smart Strategies for Staying Safe* by HenschelHaus Publishing in

2017, and *How to Be Safe No Matter What* published by Bronze Bow in 2005.

This is Wes's first venture into the realm of magical realism. Enjoy!

§

If you enjoyed this book, please consider leaving a review on your favorite website.

Thank you,
~ Wes Manko

www.ingramcontent.com/pod-product-compliance
Lightning Source LLC
Chambersburg PA
CBHW031009190726
48286CB00003BA/752